VAMPIRE DAWN

/ / / /

J.R. RAIN

THE VAMPIRE FOR HIRE SERIES

Published by
Crop Circle Books
212 Third Crater, Moon

Printed in the United States of America.

ISBN-13: 978-1548088507
ISBN-10: 1548088501

Dedication

To Scott Nicholson and Aiden James.
Great friends, great writers.

Acknowledgments

A special thank you to the following readers: Beth Lidiak, Kathy Woodard, Leslie Whitaker, Lori Lilja, Holly Sanders, Rhonda Plumhoff, Sandy Gillberg, Andrea DaSilva, Amanda Winger-Stabley, Carmen Vazquez-Rodriguez, Mary Adam-Dussel, Vicki Dussel and Michelle Craig Sanders. Thank you all for your help!

Author's Note:

The events in *Vampire Dawn* take place after *Christmas Moon*. Although my intention had been to write a fun and lighthearted holiday story featuring Samantha Moon and the gang, *Christmas Moon* ended up being, among other things, a continuation of Samantha's storyline.

—J.R. Rain

"They had forgotten the first lesson, that we are to be powerful, beautiful, and without regret."
—*Interview With a Vampire*

"I can smell the sunlight on your skin."
—*True Blood*

1.

It was early afternoon and I was vacuuming.

Others like me were, undoubtedly, sleeping contentedly in crypts or coffins or castle keeps. Me, I was vacuuming up bits of pretzels and popcorn. Last night was movie night, and the kids had picked *Captain America*, and I did my best not to drool over the bowl of popcorn I pretended to eat. Yes, I have to *pretend* to eat around my children. Since I'm unable to eat any real food, I'd become a master of hiding my food in napkins, in the bottom of sodas, and even on others' plates. More than once little Anthony had turned to look at something that I pointed at, only to discover that he had, remarkably, even *more* fries in his Happy Meal. Miracles do happen.

As I vacuumed, I caught snatches of Judge Judy wagging her finger at a cheating young man who looked like he was on the verge of tears, but then again, that could have just been wishful thinking. After all, there's something special about watching a strong woman reduce a dirtbag to tears.

Maybe it's the devil in me.

Or the cheated-on wife in me.

At any rate, I had just put away the vacuum and straightened the pillows on the couch when the doorbell rang. I flipped down my sunglasses and, after mentally preparing myself for the short blast of sunlight that I was about to experience, I opened the door.

I always gasp when I'm exposed to sunlight, and now was no exception. Even with the shades on. Even with the sunscreen I wear indoors. Even with all the layers of clothing I presently had on. I always gasp. Every time.

Standing in the doorway was a big man. Not as big as Kingsley or even my new detective friend, Jim Knighthorse, but certainly big enough. Detective Sherbet of the Fullerton Police Department was one of the few people who knew my super-secret identity. I hadn't planned on telling him what I was, but the detective was no dummy.

So I had decided to come clean, and he had proven to be a true friend. Not only had he maintained my secret, he sought my assistance.

Like now, apparently.

I absently adjusted my hair. For someone who was insecure at best, not having full use of a mirror was a major setback. Although I could make out the general shape of my face in a mirror if I was wearing enough make-up, my hair, strangely, didn't reflect.

I mean, what the hell is that all about?

I knew the answer, but that didn't make it any easier to accept. On that accursed night seven years ago when I was forever changed, my body had somehow crossed from the natural world into the supernatural world. A world where mirrors were no longer relevant.

"You look fine, Samantha," said Detective Sherbet. "Quit worrying."

I stepped aside as he moved past me. He was carrying a greasy bag that looked suspiciously like donuts. I quickly shut the door behind him.

I turned and faced him, recovering from the shock of sunlight. "Why did you say that?" I asked.

"Say what?" he asked, easing his considerable bulk down onto my new couch. The couch was one of those L-shaped deals that a mother and her two kids could get comfy in. At least, that was the theory. In practice, getting comfy with Anthony invariably meant dealing with a steady onslaught of gas.

"That thing you said about not worrying."

Sherbet was already rooting around for his first donut. "Because you sounded worried."

I leaned a shoulder against the door. "Except I didn't say anything, Detective."

Sherbet plucked a pink cake donut from the depths of the bag and, looking imminently pleased, was just bringing it to his mouth when he paused. He didn't look happy pausing. "Yes you did, Sam."

"No, I didn't."

"You were talking about your hair not growing, make-up and not seeing your hair in the mirror—and I gotta tell you, kid, you nearly bored me to tears." Now he happily resumed consuming the donut. Watching such a big man, such a distinguished man, eat a little pink donut was, well, cute.

I moved away from the door and crossed the living room, noticing for the first time a pair of Anthony's dirty skivvies jammed into the corner of the couch, maybe two feet away from Sherbet. How and why they got there would be an interesting conversation between Anthony and me later.

For now, though, I sat next to the toxic undies, so close to Sherbet that I was nearly in his lap. The big detective looked at me curiously but didn't say anything. I casually felt for the dirty skivvies, found them, wadded them up and stood. I was certain Sherbet hadn't seen me, although he was watching me curiously. Then he looked at the unfinished pink donut, turned a little green, and dropped it back into the bag, which he promptly set on the floor between his feet.

He said, "Geez, Sam. Talk about your donut buzz kill."

"What do you mean?"

"The dirty underwear talk. Look, kid, I've got a boy, too, and I've seen my fair share of skid marks.

But you sure as hell don't need to go on and on about them while a guy's trying to enjoy a donut, especially after the day I've had."

"But I didn't say anything, Detective."

"Or course you did."

"No, I didn't. Just like I didn't say anything about my hair."

"I heard it plain as day."

"No, Detective, you didn't."

He looked up at me from the new couch. There was a bit of pink frosting already caught in his thick, cop mustache. He looked at me, frowned, and then slowly wiped his mustache clean.

He said, "Your lips never moved."

"No, they didn't."

"But I heard that bit about the frosting in my mustache."

"Apparently."

"What's going on, Sam?"

"I think," I said, sitting next to him and patting him on the knee, "that you're reading my mind."

"Your mind?"

"Yes."

"Ah, hell."

2.

After a moment, Sherbet said, "What, exactly, does that mean, Samantha?"

"It means exactly that, Detective. You're reading my mind."

The detective didn't look so good. He sat forward, rubbed his eyes with a hand that was bigger than even Kingsley's. I noticed scarring on his knuckles that I had missed before. He looked down at his own knuckles, and said, "I used to be a fighter. A brawler, really. A real hothead back in the day."

"You're doing it again, Detective."

"But you said—"

"I didn't say anything."

Some of the color drained from his face. "I feel sick."

"Hang on, Detective."

I left him alone for a moment while I tossed Anthony's undies in the laundry room. When I returned, the big detective was apparently over his initial shock. He was not only holding the greasy bag of donuts, but had just consumed the last of the pink donut. All was right in the world.

"Not quite," said Sherbet, licking his fingers, but then suddenly stopped. He looked up at me. "I'm doing it again, ain't I?"

"Yes, you are."

"What's happening to me, Sam?"

I sat next to him and gave him my "penny for your thoughts" face. He smelled of Old Spice and donut grease.

I said, "You're not losing your mind, Detective. Sometimes those closest to me have access to my thoughts. I also suspect it's because you're one of the few who know what I really am. I've put a lot of trust in you. And you in me. It has something to do with that." I smiled brightly at him. "So, as you can see, having access to my thoughts is a rare privilege."

He snorted. "I feel honored." He was about to turn back to his bag of donuts when a thought occurred to him. "So does that mean you have access to my thoughts, too?"

"It does."

"I'm not sure how I feel about that."

"Don't worry, Detective. Your deep, dark secrets are safe with me. Besides, I won't access your thoughts unless you give me permission."

"Do you know how crazy that sounds, Sam?"

"I do."

"Are we both crazy?"

"Maybe."

Sherbet stared at me. He was an old-school homicide investigator. Strictly by the books. Just the facts, ma'am. Logical, rational, tough, fair, street smart. A skilled investigator. Then one day a vampire appeared in his life—granted, a cute and spunky vampire—and his neat little world came crashing down.

"I wouldn't say crashing down, Sam. Maybe turned upside down a little. And, yes, I know I'm reading your thoughts again."

I grinned. "Maybe we should get to why you're here."

He sat straighter. "Gladly. Which is an odd thing to say about a serial killer."

"He struck again," I said.

Sherbet nodded. "Corona this time."

"Drained of blood?"

He nodded. "Completely. Same M.O. Massive wound in the neck. Knife wound, we think. Bruising around the ankles. Found this one wrapped in a blanket in a ditch."

"Female?"

"Male."

"So he's alternating his kills," I said. "Male, female, male."

Sherbet thought about that. He also thought about another donut. A moment later he was pulling out a strawberry French cruller that looked all kinds of delicious.

"It will be," he said, reading my mind again without realizing it. "And I suppose the killer is. Three males, and three females. As you know, that doesn't fit the typical profile. Serial killers tend to stick to one gender."

"Unless they're after something besides kicks."

"They? You think there might be more than one killer?"

"Like you said, it doesn't fit the profile."

"Same pattern, though."

"All drained of blood," I said.

"The work of a vampire?" he said.

"The work of someone," I said. I found myself watching his every move as he worked on the cruller. Crullers had been my favorite. "Vampires don't need that much blood."

Sherbet stopped chewing. "And how much blood does a vampire need?"

"Sixteen ounces or so, every few days."

At least, that's how much were in the packets of animal blood I received monthly from the Norco butchery.

Sherbet stared at me openly, even forgetting to close his mouth as he chewed. Still, seeing the half-masticated cruller did not kill my brief donut craving. He asked, "And what happens if you don't get your blood?"

I shrugged. "I turn into a raving, blood-sucking maniac who prowls the streets looking for victims.

Prostitutes mostly, but sometimes hipsters at Starbucks, or those young guys who dance around street corners holding signs pointing to furniture stores going out of business."

"Are you quite done, Sam?"

"Quite."

He reached inside his light jacket and removed some folded papers. "Here are my notes on the latest victim. Read through them, see what you can find."

"Will do, Detective."

Months ago, when the case had turned from weird to weirder, Sherbet had hired me to be an official consultant on the case. His fellow detectives didn't like it; after all, why hire a private dick? Well, what they didn't know wouldn't kill them.

Sherbet eased his bulk off the couch and stood, knuckling his lower back. "You're one freaky chick, you know."

"Words every chick wants to hear."

He quit knuckling and looked at me with so much compassion that tears nearly came to my eyes. He reached out and pulled me in for the mother of all bear hugs. He said, "I'm sorry all this happened to you, Sam."

I hugged him back. "I know."

"You're going to be okay, kid."

"Thank you."

He stepped away. "Now, let's catch the son of a bitch who's doing this to these people."

"We will, Detective."

He seemed about to do something, then nodded and left, gripping his bag of donuts like a lifeline.

3.

At 3:30 p.m. on an overcast Tuesday afternoon, lathered in Aveeno SPF 100 sunscreen, I dashed out my door and sprinted across my front yard as if my life depended on it.

And I'm pretty sure it did.

Despite the gray skies, the thick jacket, and the layer of greasy sunscreen, my skin still felt like it was on fire. My garage is not attached. Back in the day, my ex-husband didn't think we needed an attached garage. Houses with unattached garages were cheaper.

Thanks, asshole.

Of course, little did he know that one day the sun would be my enemy and I would have to endure daily torturous mid-afternoon sprints.

Anyway, at the garage, I fumbled with the Masterlock until I got the key in and opened the sucker. I noticed my hands were already shaking and reddening. Any longer and they would begin blistering.

I'm such a freak.

I yanked open the garage door far harder than I probably should have. The thing nearly tore off its rusty tracks. Once open, I dashed inside and breathed a small sigh of relief, even though there was never really any relief for me. Not during the day, at least. Not when I should be sleeping in a dark room with the blinds pulled shut and dead to the world.

I started the van, cranked up the AC, and let it cool my burning flesh. Finally, I backed out of the garage and headed for my kids' school.

Just another day in the neighborhood.

***

After picking up the kids and spending the evening helping them with their homework, I called up a new sitter I'd been using lately, a very responsible sixteen-year-old girl. Luckily, she was available, and when she arrived, I hugged my kids and kissed them and told them to be good. Mercifully, neither shuddered at my cold touch. Cold lips, cold fingers and cold hugs were the norm in our family. Still, Anthony promptly wiped his kiss off.

"Gross, Mom," he said, never taking his eyes off his video game, giving it far more concentration than he ever did his homework. As an added precaution, he absently raised his shoulder, using it to wipe his cheek clean.

Now, with the sun mercifully far behind planet Earth, I found myself heading east on the 91 Freeway. Me, and nearly all of southern California, too. I settled in for the long commute, tempted, as usual to pull over and take flight.

Instead, I sat back and turned up the radio and tried to remember what life was like before I became what I currently am.

But I couldn't. At least, not really, and that scared the hell out of me. My new reality dominated all aspects of my life, all thoughts and all actions, and as I followed a sea of red taillights and bad drivers, I realized my humanity was slipping further and further away.

I hate when that happens.

4.

The crime scene wasn't much of a crime scene. It also wasn't too hard to find. At least, not for me.

Using Sherbet's notes, I soon found an area of road that had recently seen a lot of activity. The dirt was grooved deeply with tires, and there was even some crime scene tape left behind in one of the sage brushes.

I parked my minivan off the side of the winding road and got out. Yes, there are actually winding roads in southern California. At least, up here in these mostly barren hills. Winter rain had given life to some of the dried-out seedlings that baked during the spring, summer and fall seasons, which, out here in the high desert, was really just one long-ass summer. The stiff grass gave the hill some color, even at night. At least, to my eyes.

I shut the door and beeped it locked. Why I beeped it locked, I didn't know. I was alone up here on the hillside, parked inside a turnout, hidden in shadows and what few bushes there were.

Which made it even more remarkable that the body had even been found in the first place.

According to Sherbet's notes, a city worker making his routine rounds had come upon the body. He might not have found it, either, if not for the turkey vultures and the foul smell.

Predictably, it hadn't been a pretty sight.

Like the others, this one was rolled up in a dirty sheet and tied off on both ends. The same type of sheet, every time. A sheet commonly sold at Wal-Mart, of all places. The vultures had gotten through the sheet, using their powerful beaks. Apparently, they had made a meal of the intestines, but that's as far as they got before the worker showed up.

I had seen a handful of corpses back in my days as a federal agent. But, mercifully, I had never seen a human body eaten by vultures. I was glad Sherbet spared me the photos.

Yes, even vampires get queasy.

The air was cool and crisp. I was wearing jeans and a light jacket, although I really didn't need a jacket. I wore it because I thought it looked cute. Really, when you're as cold on the inside as the weather is on the outside, jackets are a moot point.

Unless they're cute.

The air was heavy with sage and juniper and smelled so fresh that it was easy to forget that bustling Orange County was just forty-five minutes away.

I studied the crime scene. It was a mess. What few plants there were had been trampled. Footprints everywhere. Tire prints. And deeper gouges into the earth that I knew were from the Corona mobile command. A trailer they hauled out to process evidence, or as much as they could, right there on the spot. I even found two deep ruts in the road that I seriously suspected were from a helicopter's skids. It was a wonder the rotor downdraft hadn't erased all the other tracks.

I scanned the area, looking deeper into the darkness than I had any right to see, seeing things that I probably shouldn't. I'm talking about energy. Spirit energy. Even in the desert I sense and see energy. Small explosions of light that appear and disappear. These are faint. Mere whispers.

What I wasn't seeing was perhaps more telling. There was no lost spirit here. No lost *human* spirit.

Which told me something. It told me that I was either completely insane and lost my mind years ago and was currently babbling away at some mental hospital, or that the victim had been killed elsewhere.

I was hoping it was the latter. Although, trust me, there were times I actually hoped it was the former.

Anyway, what I didn't see is the bright, static energy that often makes up a human spirit. That is, one who has once lived and passed on. The newer the spirit, the sharper they come into focus. I've gotten used to seeing such spirits these days. I'm a regular Sylvia Browne, although you won't find me on Montel Williams. At least, not yet. Maybe if he asks nicely.

Then again, I had a tendency to not show up in photographs or video.

So much for my talk show circuit, I thought, as I circled the area where the body had been found. As I did so, the wind picked up, lifting my hair, flapping my jacket.

I tried to get a feel for the land, for what had been here. For *who* had been here, but these psychic gifts of mine were relatively new and I was only getting fleeting images. One of those fleeting images was that of the body still lying undisturbed on the ground, wrapped in the dirty sheet.

I went back to the spot where the body had been found and knelt to examine the ground. There was nothing left of the crime scene, of course. The investigators had been all over it.

Most telling, there hadn't been any blood. As I knelt in this spot with my eyes closed, feeling the wind, hearing the rustle of dried leaves, I heard something else.

A voice. No, a memory of a voice. A hauntingly familiar voice. Deep and rich. Telling someone to dump the body here. Good, good. Let's go.

And that's all the psychic hits I got.

No, not quite. Another memory came to me. Another image. A snapshot, really. I saw a bag. Lying deep in a deep ravine.

Except there were damn ravines everywhere.

Hell, there were ravines within ravines. I only had to think about it for a second or two, before I started stripping out of my clothes.

Right there at the crime scene.

5.

There's nothing like being naked in the desert.

Seriously. With my clothing folded on the hood of my van, I stepped across the cool dirt, picked my way through a tangle of elderberry and carefully stepped around a patch of beavertail cactus. I moved past the general area where the body had been found and headed deeper into the empty hills.

The desert scents were heady and intoxicating. Sage and juniper and creosote. Pungent, sharp and whispery. The desert sand itself seemed to have a scent all its own, too. Something ancient that hinted at death, at life, of survival and of distant memories. This place, so close to civilization, yet so far removed, too, smelled as it had for eons, for millenniums. The sand, I knew, was sprinkled with the bones of the dead. Dead vermin, dead coyotes, dead anything and everything that ever ventured into these bleak hills.

I continued through the empty landscape. I was alone. I could sense it, see it, feel it.

I moved over springy, green grass that stood little chance once the brief winter rains ended, once the heat set in again. Southern California is mostly desert, and never is it more apparent than in these barren hills.

The moon was nearly full. *Uh oh.* That meant Kingsley would be, ah, *indisposed* for a few days.

My body felt strong. As strong as the wind that had now whipped my hair into a frenzy. Sometimes I felt elemental, too. Tied to the days and nights, to the sun and earth. Tied to blood.

Elemental.

Like a dark fairy. A dark fairy with bat wings.

I headed deeper into the desert, following a natural path that might have been a stream bed in wetter times. The rock underfoot was loose, although I rarely lost my balance. Down I went, down the slope, following the rock-strewn path, until before me a deep blackness opened up. A ravine.

I stopped, breathing in the cool, desert air, although these days I no longer needed much air. I opened and closed my hands, feeling stronger than I ever had. Then again, I always feel like that, each and every night. Stronger than I ever had.

I continued on, skirting a copse of stunted milkwoods along the edge of the ravine. I felt a pair of eyes watching me. I turned my head, looked up. There, a coyote sitting high atop a nearby boulder, eyes glowing yellow in the night. Its eyes, amazingly, like Kingsley's. Now I saw more movement from around the boulder. Heard claws clicking, scratching. More coyotes. I could smell them, too. Intoxicatingly fresh blood wafted from their musky coats. They had just feasted on a recent kill.

My stomach growled.

I cursed and moved on as the pack watched me silently, warily, keeping their distance. Soon, I reached what I had been searching for: the cliff's edge. Here, light particles swirled frenetically, seemingly caught in the updraft of wind gusts that moaned over crevasses and caves and outcroppings of rock.

My toes curled over the edge. Loose sand and rock tumbled into the ravine. Behind me, I heard the coyotes turn and leave.

I listened to the wind moving over the land, to the insects scurrying and buzzing, to my own growling stomach. I inhaled the last of the lingering, haunting scent of blood before the coyotes were too far off for even my enhanced senses.

I looked out over the ledge. The cliff dropped straight down, disappearing into blackness, although I could see an outcropping of rock about halfway down. I would have to avoid that.

I closed my eyes and exhaled slowly. If my life hadn't been so weird over these past seven years, I might have been surprised to find myself standing naked at the edge of a cliff, in the high deserts outside of Orange County.

But now weirdness was the norm, and so I just stood there, head tilted back a little, hair whipping in the wind, hands slightly outstretched, until the flame appeared in my thoughts.

Within the flame appeared something hideous... and beautiful. The creature I would become.

With that thought planted firmly in mind, I leaped from the cliff's edge and out into the night.

6.

I arched up and out.

I hovered briefly in mid-air at the apex of the arch, my arms spread wide, my hair drifting above my shoulders in a state of suspended animation.

From here, as I briefly hovered, I could see Lake Mathews sparkling under the nearly full moon. I could also see the barb wire fence, too. Only in southern California do they surround a lake with barb wire. Beyond, the cities of Corona and Riverside sparkled like so many jewels. Flawed jewels.

And then I was falling, head first, like an inverted cross. The bleak canyon walls sped past me, just feet away. Dried grass swept past me, too. Lizards scuttled for cover, no doubt confused as hell. Dry desert air blasted me, thundered over my ears.

I knew the protrusion of rock was coming up

fast.

I closed my eyes, and the creature in the flame regarded me curiously, cocking its head to one side.

Faster, I sped. My outstretched arms fought the wind.

The creature in the flame, the creature in my mind, seemed somehow closer now. And now I was rushing toward it—or it was rushing toward me. I never knew which it was.

I gasped, contorted, expanded.

And now my arms, instead of fighting the air, caught the air, used the air, manipulated the air, and now I wasn't so much falling as angling away from the cliff, angling just over the rocky protrusion. In fact, my right foot—no, the claws of my right foot —just grazed the rock. Lizards, soaking up what little heat they could from the rock, scurried wildly, and I didn't blame them.

Here be monsters.

I continued angling down, speeding so fast that by all rights I should be out of control. Wings or no wings, I should have tumbled down into the ravine below, disappearing into a forest of beavertail cactus so thick that my ass hurt just looking at them.

But I didn't crash.

Instead, I was in total control of this massive, winged body, knowing innately how to fly, how to command, how to maneuver. I knew, for instance, that angling my wings minutely would slow me enough to soar just above the beavertail, as I did now, their spiky paddles just missing my flat underside.

Yes, completely flat. In this form, I was no longer female. I was, if anything, asexual. I existed for flight only. For great distances, and great strength, too.

Now, as the far side of the canyon wall appeared before me, I instinctively veered my outstretched arms—wings—and shot up the corrugated wall, following its contours easily, avoiding boulders and roots and anything that might snag my wings or disembowel me.

Up I went, flapping hard. And with each downward thrust, my body surged faster and faster, rocketing out of the canyon like a winged missile.

In the open air, I was immediately buffeted by a strong wind blowing through the hills, but my body easily adjusted for it, and I rose higher still. I leveled off and the thick hide that composed of my wings snapped taut like twin sails.

Twin black sails. With claws and teeth.

Below, I saw dozens of yellow eyes watching me silently. I wondered just how much these coyotes knew...and whether or not they were really coyotes.

The wind was cold and strong. I was about two hundred feet up, high enough to scan dozens of acres at once, as my eyes in this form were even better, even sharper.

I was looking for the ravine that I had seen in my vision. Only a brief flash of a vision, of course, but one that remained with me, seared into my memory. In particular, I was looking for what had been tossed *into* the ravine.

No doubt, whoever had tossed it had thought the package was as good as gone. After all, even a team of policemen and state troopers couldn't cover every inch of this vast wasteland.

I flew over hills and canyons, over Lake Mathews and its barbed wire fence. High above me came the faint sound of a jet engine, and in the near distance, a Cessna was flying south. I wondered idly if I showed up on their radar, but I doubted it. After all, if I didn't show up in mirrors, why would I show up on radars?

The wind tossed me a little, but I went with it, enjoying the experience. Everything about this form was enjoyable. The land spread before me in an eternity of undulating hills and dark ravines, marching onward to the mountain chains that crisscrossed southern California. Yes, even southern California has mountains chains.

I flapped my wings casually, without effort or thought, moving my body as confidently and innately as one would when reaching for a coffee mug. I circled some more, looking for a match to the snapshot image in my head. I continued like this for another half hour or so, soaring and flapping, turning and searching. And then I came upon a hill that looked promising.

Very promising.

I descended toward it, dipping my wing, feeling the rush of wind in my face...a rush that I would never truly get used to. Or, rather, never wanted to get used to. How does one ever get used to flying? I didn't know, and I didn't want to know. I wanted the experience to always remain fresh, always new.

The hill kept looking promising, and now there was the same stunted tree that I'd seen in my vision.

I swooped lower.

There, resting next to the tree trunk and nearly impossible to see with the naked eye, was a small package. No, not quite. A bulging plastic bag.

I dropped down, circling once, twice, then landed on a smooth rock near the tree, tucking in my wings. Feeling like a monster in a horror movie, I used my left talon to snag the bag, then leaped as I high as I could, stretched out my wings, caught the wind nicely, and lifted off the ground.

A few minutes later, back at my minivan and naked as the day I was born, I opened the bag and looked inside.

"Bingo," I said.

7.

I was alone in my office with the dead man's bag.

The drive back from the hills outside of Corona had been excruciatingly long, despite the fact there had been no traffic. Excruciating, because I was itching to see inside the bag. The bag, I knew, was key evidence. I also knew that I should hand it over to Detective Sherbet ASAP. And I would. Eventually.

After I had a little looksee.

With the kids asleep and the babysitter forty bucks richer, I sat in my office and studied the still-closed bag. It was just a white plastic trash bag with red tie handles. The handles were presently tied tight. The bag itself was half full, which, on second thought, said more about my outlook on life these days than about anything in the bag.

I was wearing latex gloves since I didn't want to

ruin perfectly good evidence. To date, there had been five bodies located. Five bodies drained of blood. Sherbet had brought me on board after the fourth. Unfortunately, I hadn't been given much access to the actual evidence, despite Sherbet's high praise for me and my background as a federal investigator. Ultimately, homicide investigators still saw me as a rent-a-cop, someone not to take seriously, a private dick without a dick, as someone had once said.

Anyway, Sherbet had mostly gotten me caught up via reports and taped witness statements. Sadly, the witnesses hadn't witnessed much, and the four previous bodies had yielded little in the way of clues. And what clues the police had, they weren't giving me access to.

So, this little bag sitting in front of me represented my first—and only—direct evidence to the case.

And I wasn't about to just turn it over. At least, not yet.

So I photographed the bag from all angles, noting any smudges and marks. Once done, I carefully used a pair of scissors and clipped open the red plastic ties. I parted the bag slowly, and once fully open, I took more photos directly into the bag, carefully documenting the layout of the items within. Then I painstakingly removed each item, setting each before me and photographing them as they emerged.

All in all, there were fifteen items in the bag.

Most of the items were clothing: jeans, tee shirt, socks, shoes, underwear. There was jewelry, too, a class ring and a gold necklace. The necklace had some dried blood in it. There was blood splatter on the tee shirt, too, and the running shoes.

But, most important, there was a wallet, complete with a driver's license, credit cards, folded receipts and even a hide-a-key tucked behind the license.

"Well, well, well," I said.

In a slot behind one of the credit cards was a private investigator's wet dream: his social security number. With that, he would have no secrets from me.

His name, for starters, was Brian Meeks. He was 27 years old and even kind of cute.

But most important, the moment I began extracting items from the bag and then from the wallet, I began receiving powerful hits. Psychic hits. Haunting, disturbing, horrific hits.

I saw his life. I saw his death.

I saw his killer.

And when I finally put the items away, back into the wallet and back into the bag, I sat back in my chair and pulled my knees up to my chest and buried my face between my knees and sat like that for a long, long time.

8.

You there, Fang?

When I had caught my breath and my hands had quit shaking enough to type, I had grabbed my laptop and curled up on my new couch. The new, L-shaped couch was nearly as big as the living room itself, and that's just the way I liked it. There was enough room for some serious cuddling on here, and luckily my kids were still young enough to want to cuddle with their mommy. Even if Mommy had perpetual cold feet. Hey, if I had to put up with Anthony's farts, then they could put up with Mommy's cold feet.

A moment later, the little circular icon next to Fang's name turned green, which meant he had just signed on. Next, I saw him typing a message, as indicated by wiggling pencil in the corner of the screen.

You are upset, Moon Dance.

Fang, like Detective Sherbet, was psychically connected to me. He would know how I felt, and what I was thinking, especially if I opened myself up to him.

Very upset.

Tell me about it.

I did. Fang, like many in Orange County, knew about the drained bodies and about the serial killer. The papers were having a field day with this story, as were late-night talk-show hosts. With the world currently in the grip of Twilight mania, a real story about real bodies being drained of blood was making some national headlines. As Fang knew, I had been hired as a special consultant to the case, I simply caught him up to date on tonight's adventures. I also caught him up on the psychic hits I'd received.

He was hanging upside down?

Yes.

And he never got a good look at his killer?

No. I think he had been rendered unconscious. I only got a sensation of him returning to consciousness.

And when he did, he was hanging upside down?

Yes.

Fang wrote: *What else did he see before he was, you know...*

Killed?

Yes.

I rubbed my head as the images, now forever imprinted into my brain, appeared in my thoughts again. I wrote: *He didn't get a good look. He was swinging wildly upside down, trying to break free.*

His hands were tied?

I think so, yes.

And he saw only one man?

Maybe two. Hard to know. That's when he started screaming.

And that's when the knife appeared, wrote Fang.

Yes, I wrote, feeling drained, despite this being the middle of the night.

And they cut his throat, wrote Fang.

Yes.

This doesn't sound like a vampire.

No, I wrote.

It sounds like a sick son of a bitch.

I waited before replying. Finally, I wrote: *There's more, Fang. I saw...other bodies. At least two more. Both hanging upside down.*

Jesus, Sam.

They were suspended over a tub of some sort.

A tub?

Yes.

They were collecting the blood, Fang wrote.

That's what I think, too.

But why?

I thought about it for only a moment before I wrote: *If I had to guess, I would say that he supplies blood for vampires.*

9.

Kingsley was waiting for me outside Mulberry Street Restaurant in downtown Fullerton.

He looked dashing and massive, and I think my whole body sighed when he smiled at me. A big, toothy smile. Confident smile. Deep dimples in his cheeks. His ears even moved a little. The way a dog's might. He was wearing a scarf that matched his eyes and I think I might have mewed a little. Like a kitten.

"Hello, beautiful," he said, smiling even bigger.

"Hello, Mr. Observant," I said, grinning, and came to him. He wrapped a strong arm around my lower waist and pulled me into him, lifting me a little off my feet. I wasn't entirely sure he knew he had lifted me off my feet. One moment I was standing there, the next my heels were free of any gravitational pull.

He set me down again. "God, you smell good."

"For a dead girl?"

"You're very much alive."

"Well, that's good news."

He planted a big, wet kiss on my lips that I didn't want to end. At least, not for the next two or three hours. When we separated, I noticed an old man watching us. Hell, I would have watched us, too.

"You hungry?" asked Kingsley. I noticed his five o'clock shadow was looking more like a three-day growth. The surest indicator that a full moon was rising.

"Hungry enough to suck you dry," I said.

Now he shivered. "With talk like that, we might just skip dinner."

We were seated immediately at our favorite table near the front window. The waiters here knew my preferences and, after giving us one of their finest white wines—one of the few non-hemoglobic beverages I can enjoy—they brought us our meals. Salmon for Kingsley. Steak for me. Rare.

Very, very rare.

Rather than use a knife and fork, I used a spoon, and, as casually as I could, I dipped it into the warm blood that had pooled around the meat and brought it to my lips. I tried not to feel like the ghoul that I was.

Just a girl with her man, I told myself. A man, of course, who just so happened to be bigger than most men. And far hairier. Especially at this time of the month.

Kingsley, suffering from no such eating restrictions, went to work on the salmon. Although the defense attorney dressed immaculately, he ate like a pig. And, yeah, I was jealous as hell.

The waiter came by and filled my wine glass. Since I had taken precisely three sips, the filling part didn't take long. Kingsley ordered another beer, and when the waiter was gone, I said to him, "I found another medallion."

"Another what?" he mumbled around his salmon. Or, rather, I *think* he said.

"Medallion. You know, like the one before. But this one is inlaid with emerald roses, rather than ruby."

Kingsley's lips were shiny with grease. His impossibly full lips. His longish hair hung just below his collar. He was the picture of the maverick attorney, who just so happened to look like a ravenous wolf, too. "Tell me about it," he said.

And I did. I told him about the case I had taken on around Christmas, a case in which I had helped a sweet man find a family heirloom, of sorts. A sweet man who just so happened to be a hoarder, too. For payment, I was permitted to pick anything I wanted from his piles of junk. I had cheated. I had used my intuition to hone in on something particularly valuable, something that had lain hidden and mostly forgotten under piles of crap.

A box. With a medallion.

A medallion that was a near-exact replica of the one I had owned six months ago. And that medallion had contained powerful magicks. So powerful, in fact, that it had reversed vampirism.

"So the question is," I said. "Can this medallion do the same?"

During my recounting, Kingsley had finished his salmon and was now working on his cubed rosemary potatoes. The fork in his hand looked miniature. "Do you have the medallion with you now?" he asked.

I did. I showed it to him. Kingsley immediately frowned. A frown for Kingsley meant his bushy eyebrows came together to form one long incredibly bushy eyebrow. "You should have left it at home," he said, glancing around.

"And miss seeing your bushy eyebrows come together?"

"I'm serious, Sam. Stuff like this..." he lowered his voice. "You, of all people, know the lengths some people—"

"Or vampires."

His long eyebrow quivered. "Yes, Sam. Vampires. Some vampires will kill—"

"And kidnap."

"Yes, and kidnap for these things."

I set it on the table and mostly covered it with my hand. "And what is this thing? Another immortality reverser?"

Kingsley shook his head sharply. "No. There was only one of those made."

"And you know this how?"

"I know some things," he said.

"Because you've been around longer than me."

"A lot longer than you, Sam."

"Fine. So only one of those were made. Then what's this?" I moved my hand aside, revealing the shining medallion again. It caught the overhead chandelier light and returned a thousandfold, and the three emeralds within twinkled like green stars. Or like lime jello. Which so happened to be Anthony's and Tammy's favorite jello.

Kingsley glanced briefly at the medallion before reaching across the table and covering my hand with his own. Hell, he covered most of my wrist, too. And some of my napkin and plate. Big hands.

"I don't know yet," he said. "But I can tell you one thing."

"And what's that?"

"It's valuable as hell. Which means..." And his voice trailed off.

Unfortunately, I knew the ending to this sentence all too well. "Which means some people will kill for it."

"Some people," said Kingsley, "or some vampires."

10.

"You tampered with evidence. What were you thinking, Sam?" scolded Detective Sherbet.

"I was thinking about finding our killer."

We were in his glass office. Some of the officers on duty were watching us from outside the office. One or two were shaking their heads in a way that suggested they did not approve of me or of the department using my inferior services.

"Your men don't like me," I said.

"They see it as a slap in the face, a blow to their ego," said Sherbet, sitting back in his chair. He laced his thick fingers over his rotund belly. The rotund belly was looking a little more rotund these days. This time, however, I shielded my thoughts from him. He didn't need to know what I thought of his belly. He went on, "They don't understand why I brought you in, so they see you as a sort of indictment on their own abilities."

"If they only knew," I said.

"Truth is, sometimes I wish I didn't know, Sam. I mean, isn't this kind of stuff supposed to just be in books and movies?"

I said, "Someone told me recently that if enough people believe in something, put their attention on something, then that something becomes a reality."

Sherbet immediate shook his head. "That doesn't make sense," he said, which didn't surprise me much. Detectives lived and died by things that made sense. Cold hard facts. "Who told you this?"

"My guardian angel. Actually, my ex-guardian angel."

Sherbet blinked. "Please tell me you're kidding."

"Sadly, no. He visited me over Christmas. Expressed his undying love for me, in fact."

"Please stop. There's only so much I can handle." Sherbet massaged his temples. "We sound crazy, you know."

"Maybe we are," I said.

"Crazy, I can accept. Guardian angels, not so much. Can I really read your mind, Sam?"

"Yes."

"And you can read my mind?" he asked.

"If I wanted to."

"My head hurts, Sam."

"I imagine it does."

He looked at me some more. As he did so, his jowls quivered a little. His nose was faintly red. "How do you do it?" he finally asked.

I didn't have to be a mind reader to know what *it* was. I said, "One day at a time. One minute at a time."

"If it were me, I would go bugfuck crazy."

We were quiet some more. The smell of coffee seemed to permanently hang suspended in the air of his office, although I could see no coffee cups. Outside his glass office wall, I could hear phones ringing, phones being answered, the rapid typing on keyboards.

"Back to you tampering with evidence," said Sherbet. "Officially, I have to ask you to never do that again."

"And unofficially?"

"Unofficially, I have to ask you what you learned."

"He's not a vampire," I said. "At least, I don't think he is."

"Then what is he? Why does he drain the bodies of blood?"

"Think of him as a supplier."

"A supplier? Of what? Blood?"

"Yes."

"For who?"

I didn't say anything. I let the detective think this through. As he studied me, I glanced around his small office. There was a picture of his wife next to his keyboard, a lovely woman I'd met just this past Christmas, a woman who was easily twenty years younger than Sherbet.

You go, Detective.

Finally, he said, "Are you implying he supplies blood to...vampires?"

"Maybe. I don't know for sure."

"Which begs the question: where do vampires get their blood?"

"We get it from all over, Detective. I get mine, as you know, from a local butchery."

"Animal blood."

"Right."

"So, this guy supplies human blood."

"Right."

"Have you ever heard anything like that, Sam?"

"Not quite like that."

"What have you heard?"

"That some people act as donors."

"Willing donors?"

"Some of them," I said.

"And some not so willingly?"

"Would be my guess," I said.

Sherbet started shaking his head, and he didn't quit shaking it until he spoke again. Finally, he said, "So, what else do you know about our killer?"

"He's got blue eyes."

"That's it?"

"That's it."

"No other psychic hits?"

"He hangs the bodies upside down to drain."

"Like a butcher."

"Yes," I said.

"Which makes sense if he's a blood supplier; after all, he wouldn't want to waste a single drop."

"Blood is money," I said.

"Jesus. Where did he kill his victims?"

I shook my head. "Hard to know. Brian Meeks regained consciousness while hanging upside down."

"Jesus," he said again. "And you saw this, what, through his eyes? From touching his stuff?"

"That's how it seems to work."

"Do you have any fucking idea how crazy we sound?"

"Some idea," I said.

Sherbet shook his head. "Did he—or you—see anything else while he was hanging upside down?"

"Yes."

"Don't say it, Sam," said Sherbet, and I think he caught a glimpse of my thoughts.

"More bodies," I said.

"I asked you not to say it."

11.

With the body now identified and most of the Fullerton Police Department looking deeply into Brian Meeks's personal and professional life, Detective Sherbet had asked me to lay low for a while and let his boys think they were doing some actual work.

I told him no problem, smiled warmly, and promptly looked into Brian Meeks's personal and professional life.

Since I knew the cops were currently turning his small apartment upside down, looking for anything and everything that could help identify the killer, that left his professional life.

Which is why I found myself outside the Fullerton Playhouse. Turns out that Brian Meeks had been an actor here in Fullerton, working primarily with local theater and community colleges. Which might explain why he lived in a one-bedroom apartment.

The Fullerton Playhouse is located on Commonwealth, near the Amtrak train station, and near what had been one of my favorite restaurants, back when my diet wasn't so one-dimensional. The Olde Spaghetti House will always have a special place in my heart. The fact that I would never again eat mizithra cheese spaghetti again was a crime in and of itself.

I parked in the mostly empty parking lot next to the wooden playhouse. A marquee sign out front read, "Elvis Has *Not* Left the Building: The Musical." Under the sign were the words: "The King is Back!"

Boy, was he ever. Last year, while searching for a missing little girl, I had teamed up with, among others, an investigator from Los Angeles. An investigator from whom I had received a very strange psychic hit. An investigator who vaguely looked and sounded like the King himself.

Turned out, the old guy had secrets of his own, secrets I would take with me to my grave, whenever the hell that might be.

Now as I sat in the parking lot in my minivan, shrinking away from the daylight, I closed my eyes and cleared my mind and cast my thoughts out and directed them toward the theater. Yes, I was getting good at this sort of thing.

Now, as my thoughts moved through the theater, I could see various people working together in small groups or individually. Actors and stage hands and set designers, anyone and everyone needed to put on a show.

So far, no hit. Nothing that made me take notice.

I pushed past the main stage to the backstage. Still nothing. I meandered down a side hallway and into a storage room. Props were everywhere. Rows upon rows of wardrobes hung from racks and hangers. Still nothing. I was about to snap back into my body when something appeared at the back of the theater.

A shadow.

It appeared suddenly from the far wall, scurried up to the ceiling, then down a side wall, then huddled in a dark corner, where it waited. I sensed that it always waited, that it was always afraid.

I shivered. Jesus, what the hell was that thing? I'd seen my fair share of ghosts and spirits, but never a shadow. Never this.

And it came from the mirror hanging from the back wall. No, not the mirror. Behind the mirror. There was a doorway there. A hidden doorway.

I tried to push through the secret door, but I was just too far away. My range is limited, and I was at the far end of it.

I snapped back into my body and, briefly disoriented, gave myself a few moments to get used to seeing through my physical eyes again. The sun was still out, which meant that the next few moments were not going to be very fun. When I had mentally prepared myself, I took a deep breath and threw open my minivan door. I dashed across the parking lot, keeping my head down, leaping over cement parking curbs like a horse at a steeplechase.

When I finally ducked under the marquee and into the blessed shade, I was gasping and clutching my chest and maybe even whimpering a little. The sun was truly not my friend. And that was a damn shame.

When the burning subsided enough for me to think straight, I pushed my way into the theater's main entrance.

12.

The theater looked much the same as it had in my thoughts, except for the details.

The same crew was on stage, hammering and sawing away on a wooden cut-out of a pink Cadillac. The same group of actors were going over lines off to the left of the stage.

No one noticed me. No one cared. And why should they? They were all busy putting on a stage show about Elvis, and what could be cooler than that?

With murder cases, you always interviewed those closest to the victims, then worked your way out. I would let the police interview any family members, although precious few showed up in my preliminary research. Still, most people tended to open up to an official murder investigation. Not everyone opened up to private eyes.

Go figure.

So as I stood there and surveyed the darkened theater, watching workers carry props and pull cables, actors read and re-read lines, and various stage hands in group meetings, I realized why I was here. Why I had jumped the gun and come here on my own. Against Sherbet's wishes, no less.

He's here, I thought. *The killer is here.*

Before me, the stadium seating sloped downward. The Fullerton Playhouse wasn't huge. I would guess that it could seat maybe one thousand. The seating itself was arranged into four quadrants, with two aisles leading down and aisles on each side. I was standing on a platform near a metal railing. Wheelchair seating, if my guess was correct. Various lights were on throughout the theater, but certainly not all of them, as much of the seating was in shadows.

A quick count netted me twenty-four people. And one of them was the killer. I was sure of it.

How I knew this, I no longer questioned or doubted, and as I stood there scanning the theater, I felt that something was off. And I was pretty sure I knew why.

There was more than one killer.

It takes a certain kind of personality to be an actor, or even hang around the theater. You had to love masks, the ability to pretend to be something other than what you were. Which was a pretty useful trait for a killer, too.

As I stepped forward, a small man appeared out of the shadows to my left. Holding a clipboard and mumbling to himself, he nearly ran into me before looking up. He was exactly an inch taller than me.

I held out one of my business cards. "Hi. My name's Samantha Moon, and I'm looking into the murder of Brian Meeks."

He looked at the card and blinked twice. "Are you with the police?"

"I'm a private investigator." One of the stipulations with Sherbet was that I was never, ever, to state that I was working with the police. It was a gray area he wanted to avoid. My official employer was the City of Fullerton. In fact, my checks had been issued by the city clerk's office.

"Working for whom?"

"An interested party."

He finally took my card. "What are they interested in?"

"Finding the killer." I tried not to be sarcastic, because that never helps. What did he think, the cops wanted to know his favorite picks to win the Oscars? "Can I ask you a few questions about Brian Meeks?"

He looked at my card, looked at me, looked over at the stage. I sensed his hesitation, his pain, and finally his resolve. "Okay, but only for a few minutes. We're putting on a show in a few days. Opening night. Crazy as Lady Macbeth here."

"Gotcha. We'll hurry this along. Did Brian Meeks work here as an actor?"

"For a few years now."

"Did you know him personally?"

"Not necessarily personally, but professionally. Then again, in the world of theater, personal and professional lines tend to get blurred. We're all so close."

"I bet. Are you an actor?"

"Director only."

"Gotcha. Did you direct anything Brian was in?"

He nodded. "Our last show, *Twelfth Night*. Brian was supposed to be in this new show, but..."

"He's been missing."

The little director rubbed his face. "Right. Missing. Until we heard the news this morning that he was found dead. Murdered."

"Did Brian have many friends?"

"Funny you should ask...I was just trying to think who his close friends were. I was thinking of doing some sort of memorial for him. Something either before or after our opening show this weekend..."

"And?"

"And I couldn't think of anyone who had been close to him."

"Is that common for an actor?" I asked.

"Actually, no. We don't get many loners in this business. Extroverts, yes."

I skipped the questions of whether or not Brian had any enemies. Whoever had done this to him was doing the same thing to many people. I doubted a personal vendetta had anything to do with his death. I asked, "Had there been any other strange occurrences in this theater?"

"Strange, how?"

"Has anyone reported seeing anything...odd or unusual?"

"Not that I can think of. But a theater is a pretty odd place anyway."

"How long have you worked here?"

He looked again at the stage. I could see that a few people were waiting for him. "Five years. Worked my way up as a lighting guy out of college."

"Good for you. Who owns the theater?"

He pointed to a man sitting on a foldout chair on stage. The only man, apparently, not doing anything. "Robert Mason."

"The actor?"

"The one-time actor. His soap opera days are over. This is where he spends most of his time."

"May I have your name?" I asked.

"Tad Biggs."

I nodded and somehow kept a straight face. I said, "May I ask what's in your back room?"

"Back room?"

"Yes, the storage room at the far end of the hallway."

He blinked. Twice. No, three times. "How do you know about the storage room?"

"I'm a heck of an investigator."

"That room is strictly off limits."

"Why?"

This time he didn't blink. This time, he just

stared at me. "Because Robert Mason says it is. Look, I gotta go. We have a show to put on. I hope you guys catch the sick son of a bitch who did this to Brian."

I nodded and watched him hurry off. Then I flicked my eyes over to where Robert Mason was sitting in the foldout chair on stage—and gasped when I saw him staring back at me.

He was still as handsome as ever. Older, granted, but one hell of a handsome man. He stared at me some more, then looked away.

I shivered, and exited stage left.

13.

I was watching them from the parking lot.

Not exactly the best seat in town, granted, but it would have to do. Lately, I seemed to be almost completely intolerant to the sun. Brief sojourns were excruciating, even when I was fully clothed and lathered.

And so, while my son played soccer, I sat alone in my van, huddled in the center of my seat, thankful for the surrounding tinted glass. Of course, from where I sat, I couldn't see the entire playing field, but beggars can't be choosers.

It was a crisp late winter day, warm for this time of year, perfect for anyone who wasn't me. Before me were some bleachers filled with moms and dads and relatives and friends. The mothers all seem to know each other and they laughed and pointed and cupped their hands and shouted encouragement. They shared stories and drinks and sandwiches and chips.

I sat alone and watched them and tried not to feel sorry for myself. Easier said than done.

From where I sat, I couldn't tell who was winning, so I just watched Anthony as he ran up and down the field, disappearing and reappearing from around poles and bleachers and hedges.

From what I could tell, he had real talent, but what did I know? These days, he almost always scored a goal—sometimes even two or three. He seemed to have the strongest leg—kicking leg, that is—and a real nose for the action; at least, he was always right in the thick of things. Mostly I cringed and winced when I watched him, praying he would be careful. My overprotectiveness wasn't a surprise, especially when you consider what I went through seven months ago.

Presently, the action was coming toward my end of the field, and I sat forward in my seat. Anthony was leading the charge, elbowing his way through a crowd of kids who clearly didn't seem as athletic. And now Anthony was mostly free, pursued by opponents on either side. Amazingly, Anthony pulled away from them. Not only running faster than them, but running faster while kicking a soccer ball.

Then he reared back and kicked a laser shot into the far corner of the net, blowing it past the outmatched goalie.

Anthony's teammates high-fived him. Parents stood and cheered. I shouted and stamped my feet in the minivan. No one heard me cheer, of course. Especially not Anthony.

Still, I cheered alone from inside the minivan, rocking it all the way down to its axles. And when I was done cheering, done clapping, I buried my face in my hands and tried to forget just what a freak I was.

After the game, as parents and grandparents hugged their excited and dirty kids, I saw Anthony coming toward me. Alone, and perhaps dirtiest of all. One of the other mothers saw him and asked him something. He pointed to me sitting in the minivan. She nodded and smiled and waved to me. I waved back. She then gave Anthony a big hug and congratulated him, no doubt on playing a great game. By my count, Anthony had scored three goals. She gave him another hug and set him free.

That should be me hugging him, I thought. *That should be me walking him off the field.*

There was blood along his knees and elbows. The kid had taken a beating scoring those three goals. But he didn't limp; in fact, he didn't seem fazed by the injuries at all.

Tough kid.

He flashed me a gap-toothed smile, and my heart swelled with all kinds of love. Now he was running toward me, his cleats clickity-clacking over the asphalt. He looked like an athlete. A natural athlete. His movements fluid and easy, covering the ground effortlessly, cutting through cars and people with precision. On a dime. By the time he reached the minivan he was sprinting. He skidded to a halt and yanked open the door.

"Mom!" he shouted. "I scored three goals today!"

"Incredible!"

He jumped in and lunged across the console and gave me a big hug. The strength in his arms was real. He nearly tore me out of my seat. "Did you see them?"

"Some of them," I said. Two, in fact. Both scored on this side of the field. "So when did you get so darn good?"

He shrugged. "I dunno. Lucky, I guess."

But something suddenly occurred to me. Anthony hadn't been very good just a year ago. In fact, I distinctly recall him coming back to the van crying, wanting to quit his team. Now he was coming back to the van as the hero of the game.

And not just a hero, but clearly the best athlete on the field.

I was about to say that luck had nothing to do with it when I looked down at his legs. The cuts I had seen just a minute earlier were...gone. Only dried blood remained. And only a little bit of dried blood.

I think my heart might have stopped.

"Anthony, how do you feel?"

"Great! We won!"

"Yes, I know, but do you feel...sunburned at all?"

"Sunburned?" Distracted, he waved to a friend

passing by the van.

"Yes, sunburned or sick?"

"I feel good, Mom. I promise. Stop worrying about me."

I bit my lip and somehow managed to hide my concern. "Are you hungry, baby?"

"Duh. Of course I'm hungry."

"Of course. What do you want?"

"Duh, hamburgers!"

"Of course," I said, backing the minivan up. "Duh."

14.

You there, Fang?

I'm always here for you, Moon Dance.

Except when you're not.

Hey, a man's gotta work. What's on your mind, sweet cheeks?

Sweet cheeks?

Oops, did I write that out loud?

You did.

My bad. So what's on your mind, sugar butt?

Oh brother. I grinned, shook my head, then quickly turned somber. *There's something going on with my son.*

Is everything okay?!

Yes. I mean, I don't know.

He's not sick again, is he?

No. In fact, quite the opposite.

I told him about the healing in Anthony's leg, and my son's seemingly increased athletic ability.

There was a long pause before Fang wrote back.

Maybe you are mistaken, Moon Dance. Is it possible that his blood had already dried?

I shook my head, aware that I was alone in my living room and no one could see me shaking my head.

No. I saw the fresh wounds. My eyes happen to be very, very good.

I projected the image I had in my mind. My own memory, in fact.

A moment later, Fang wrote: *We used to call those strawberries. Probably got them sliding over the grass and maybe on some dirt.*

Right, I wrote. *And even if it had been dried blood, where was the wound?*

There was no wound?

None.

Just dried blood?

Yes.

There was another long pause, followed by *And the dried blood was recent?*

Of course. It wasn't there when I dropped him off.

Is there a chance it wasn't his blood?

No. I saw the abrasions.

In the image you projected to me, wrote Fang, *I'm pretty sure I see them, too.*

We're weird, I wrote.

Yes we are, Moon Dance. A very good kind of weird.

So what does this mean with my son?

I don't know, Moon Dance. There was another pause. *And you say he's getting better in sports, too?*

Much, much better.

Supernaturally better?

Last year about this time he was benched for picking his nose. Now he's the leading scorer. I wouldn't have thought anything about this, except...

Except when you combine it with the disappearing wound...

Right, I wrote. *There's something weird going on with my son. Fang, could you...*

I'll look into it, Moon Dance.

Thank you, Fang.

And as we were about to sign off, I caught a fleeting glimpse into Fang's mind, a thought that I was certain I wasn't supposed to see or hear. Except it wasn't so much a thought as a feeling.

Fang was hoping that if he helped me, I would help him in return. To do what, I didn't know.

But I could guess.

15.

I was in bed with Kingsley.

Not a bad place to be. Ever. It was the day after his "change" and he was feeling particularly, ah, ravenous. And not just for food. Yes, he had prepared a delicious meal for himself, and supplied me with a particularly fresh goblet of hemoglobin.

We had spent the evening in his kitchen, drinking and eating over his counter, while he looked at me with yellowish eyes that suggested that he was not only going to tear my clothing off my back, but he was going to do so in a particularly inspired way.

He didn't tear off my clothes. But they did come off quick enough, and we spent the next few hours putting our immortal bodies to good use. Very good use.

Now, we were both lying on our sides, naked

and talking quietly. The lights were off but I could see every square inch of Kingsley's epic body, which I never really got used to. It was like lying next to a small land mass, a living peninsula. Hard, corrugated, with peaks and valleys and forests and plains. Epic, immovable, sexy as hell.

I knew he could see every curve of mine, too, being a fellow creature of the night. That he could see every curve of mine gave me some degree of anxiety. I might be immortal, but I was insecure as hell about my naked body.

Kingsley, not so much. He liked to be naked. Lucky for him, I liked when he was naked, too. Presently, his shaggy hair hung down to the bed sheet, a bed sheet that was still soaked with our sweat. His relaxed bicep still looked bigger than my waist. His chest hair was thicker than normal thanks to his beastly visitor from the night before.

Yes, the big oaf was shedding all over the place. Additionally, his eyes were glowing more yellow than normal, also a residue of his recent transformation.

"Kingsley," I said.

He was presently running a thick finger over my hip. "Yeah, babe?"

"Are there really...things living inside us?"

His finger stopped on my waist. "That's not exactly bedroom talk, Sam."

"Sorry, but it's been bugging me."

"Since you met your guardian angel?"

I nodded, which looked more like a shake since

my head was propped up on my hand. The lights were out in the room, and only the silver glow from the still-mostly full moon bathed our naked bodies. "He kind of freaked me out."

"He was trying to freak you out, Sam. And he's certainly not a guardian angel. Not anymore."

"A fallen angel," I said.

"Right," said Kingsley. "Something like that."

"I spoke to whatever's in you," I said. "He said you were his vehicle to gain entrance into the mortal world again."

"So you said before. Remind me to kick his ass if I ever meet him."

I tried to smile. Mostly, I was successful. I said, "Do you feel him inside you?"

"Not really, Sam. Then again, I don't necessarily feel much when I change."

"Do you feel anything?"

"I feel anger and hate and blind rage."

"But you didn't attack me in my room last year."

"No."

"Why not?"

"Because I knew it was you."

"But did you want to attack me?"

"A part of me did. Very badly."

"But you resisted," I said.

"With all my strength and will."

"What would have happened if you attacked me?" I asked.

"We wouldn't be here now."

"Because I would be dead."

"No...you would have survived. And I would have survived, too. Vampires are as strong or stronger than even a full-blown werewolf. I'm not sure our relationship would have survived."

I shrugged. I hadn't thought of that. I said, "So, I'm as strong as you?"

"Don't sound so pleased, but yes. Although my size factors into things, I would say you are particularly strong, even for a vampire."

"Why is that?"

"I don't know. There's something going on with you that I haven't quite put a finger on."

"Oh, you put a finger on it."

He laughed. A sharp bark that startled me. "Anyway, even your everyday vampire at full power is nearly unstoppable."

"But you stopped Dominique," I said, referring to the events of seven months ago, when my son had been dying and I had faced down a particularly old and desperate vampire.

"I said nearly," said Kingsley. "That night could have quickly gone south for me."

I patted his hearty chest. I could have been slapping a side of beef. "Then it's a good thing you're such a big boy."

"Big has its benefits."

I rolled my eyes. "Please not another penis reference."

"Fine. I won't refer to my big penis."

"Oh, God. *Annnny*way, I still can't imagine

anyone—vampires or otherwise—being able to stop you."

He chuckled lightly, then studied me for a few seconds. "Actually, you could, Sam."

I snorted. "I doubt it."

"You are stronger than you realize. In fact, rumor has it that a Mr. Captain Jack was perhaps the strongest vampire of them all. That is, until you came around."

Kingsley was referring to a missing-child case that had led me to an Indian casino in Simi Valley, where a young girl's blood was being siphoned by a particularly sick son of a bitch.

Kingsley went on, "From what I understand, most others in the vampire world steered clear of Captain Jack. And look what you did to him."

"I was lucky. I had help."

"But who's alive, Sam? You vanquished a powerful vampire. You are not one to mess with."

The talk was getting a little serious, especially since we were both naked in bed. I ran a finger through his tangle of chest hair. "Then what were you doing just a few moments ago?"

He reached over and pulled me close to his superheated body. "Oh, I wasn't messing with you, Sam." And now he flipped me over onto my back and climbed on top of me. "I was making love to you."

I blinked. Hard. This was news to me. "Love?"

"Oh, yeah, Sam." He lowered his face to my skin. "Love."

At least, that's what I think he said. His words might have been a little muffled.

16.

It was early afternoon and I was at the Cal State Fullerton library.

I waved to my cute friend working behind the help desk. He smiled brightly and rose from his chair, but I breezed past, blew him a kiss, and hurried into one of the elevators going up. At the third floor, I wound my way through a maze of book aisles until I came upon the special collections room.

Cal State Fullerton had many special collections. In the science fiction wing, there was a room devoted solely to local science fiction authors. One could find original *Dune* manuscripts by Frank Herbert along with his personal notes. My favorite was the Philip K. Dick room. The world at large thought the man had a screw loose, and maybe he did. But I happened to think he was onto something. Or something was onto him.

Anyway, this was the Occult Reading Room, which consisted of extremely rare manuscripts. Like with the science fiction room, these books couldn't be checked out. Only admired. Or feared. And, yes, there were one or two books in here that definitely aroused some fear. Okay, a lot of fear.

Except today I wasn't here to read books, or even to peruse the shelves. I was here to meet a young man. A young man who, I suspected, wasn't so young.

I hung a right into the Occult Reading Room and wasn't too surprised to see that it was empty. Well, empty of anything living, that is. A very old man in spirit form sat in one of the chairs and appeared to be deep in thought. Then again, most ghosts appeared to be in deep thought. As I came in, he looked up at me, startled, frowned grumpily, and promptly disappeared into the nether-sphere.

Well, excuse me.

The reading room was really a library unto itself. It had its own shelves, its own filing system, its own desks and reading chairs. Even its own help desk, where I rang the little bell.

As I waited, I could hear something scratching from deeper within the reading room, followed by some whispering and even the occasional moan. I shivered. Creepy as hell.

A young man soon appeared from the back offices. What he did back there, I didn't know. Who he was, exactly, I didn't know that either. For all the world, he appeared as just another handsome college student with a bright smile.

His name was Archibald Maximus, and I suspected that Cal State Fullerton, unbeknownst to the students and faculty, housed perhaps one of the world's most dangerous collections of arcane and rare books, books full of dark power. Books that could do great harm in the hands of the wrong person.

I suspected young Archibald Maximus, or Max, was a gatekeeper of sorts. A watcher. A protector.

His particularly bright aura suggested I might be onto something. Although not as bright as the angel I'd met last month, Max's aura was damn bright. So much so, that it suggested he wasn't entirely of this world.

Or I could be as crazy as a loon.

"Hello, Samantha," he said, smiling, reaching across the counter and taking both of my hands in his, as a grandfather might do with his grandchild.

"You remembered my name," I said, looking from his slightly pale, but quite warm, hands. I briefly reveled in the warmth.

His eyes twinkled. "How could I forget?"

His name was Archibald Maximus, and, yes, he sounded more like a Greek god than a young librarian. Somehow, I suspected it was closer to the former than the latter.

Anyway, this was one of the rare times that I didn't worry about my cold flesh. Archibald, after all, was very aware of who I really was.

When I was done acting like a bashful

schoolgirl, I opened the box I'd been carrying with me and presented the contents to Archibald. He silently held up my newest medallion and let some of the muted light play off its golden surface. The three emerald roses sparkled with what I was certain was supernatural intensity. As he studied it, I heard something call my name from deeper within the reading room, near where I knew some of the darker books were shelved. I gasped.

"Ssssister," the voices whispered, melding into one slithering, slippery sound.

"Ignore them," said Maximus, as he continued to study the medallion.

"Ssssister Moon...come to us."

The hair on my arms stood on end. "They know my name," I said.

"Yes."

"Who are they?"

"Bound spirits."

"Bound in the books?"

He nodded without looking at me. "Yes. Waiting for someone to release them."

I shivered again. "They sound...evil."

He looked at me sharply and the merriment in his bright eyes briefly faded. Then he gave me a lopsided grin. "It's why I'm here, Sister Moon," he said. But before I could respond to that, he plunged forward, somewhat excitedly, waving the medallion. "You seem to have a penchant for attracting rare artifacts."

"How rare?"

"The rarest. Hang on..."

He moved lithely around the center help desk, swept past me, and headed deeper into the reading room. I noted that the whisperings stopped in his presence. While I watched from the help desk, he used a step stool to fetch a thick book along the upper shelves. No, not the upper shelves...it was resting *on top* of the shelf. No one would have known it was there. No one but him.

He came back a moment later, blowing dust off what appeared to be leather skin, but with an odd yellow tint to it. "Is that leather?" I asked.

He set the heavy book down in front of me and, as more dust billowed up, looked deep into me. "Not quite, Samantha. This is human skin."

"Eww."

"Eww is right," he said, but that didn't stop him from eagerly cracking open the oversized book. "Human skin makes a surprisingly suitable book cover, as you can see. Pliable without breaking."

"Eww again."

Fighting back a dry heave or two, I did my best to ignore the yellowish edges of the book and watched as Max carefully turned what I knew to be a different kind of skin. Vellum, or lamb skin. I had, after all, read *The Historian*. You can't help come out of that book a minor expert on ancient bookbinding.

Anyway, Max was working his way slowly through what appeared to be a very old book filled with wonderfully ornate and colorful drawings.

Page after page of strange-looking creatures, symbols and coded drawings. Finally, he stopped at a page containing four drawings, two of which looked very familiar.

"My medallions," I said.

"Yes," he said. "Two of them."

Indeed, there were the medallions with the ruby and emerald inlaid roses. Also pictured were medallions inlaid with sapphire and diamond roses.

"Who wrote this book?" I asked.

He looked up at me and a very strange grin appeared on his handsome face. "Me."

"But it's centuries old."

"I do good work."

"But...who are you?"

He held my gaze for a heartbeat longer, and his bright green eyes, I knew, somehow looked deeply into my soul. What it found there—or *who* it found there—I may never know. But after a moment, he said simply, "Hey, I'm just a simple librarian."

"Bullshit. That's like saying I'm just another mom."

"But isn't that also true, Samantha? Do not many things define you?"

"So, you really are a librarian?"

"In part." He reached over and patted my hand warmly, then turned his attention back to the ancient text. I noted that his nail, unlike mine, was round and smooth and very human-looking. He said, "There are four known medallions in the world, Sam. You have now possessed two."

"Who made the medallions?"

"We're not sure, but we suspect whoever *initiated* your race."

"You mean whoever created vampires."

"Yes."

"And who's *we*?"

Archibald Maximus smiled at me from behind the counter. Our faces, I noted, were a mere eight inches apart as we both hovered over the old book. He could have been just another college student working his way through school. Could have been. But wasn't.

"Others like me, Samantha."

"Other...librarians?"

He dipped his head a little. "Yes, something like that."

I suddenly had an impression in my thoughts of various old souls positioned around the world, fighting a fight that few knew existed, and fewer still would ever believe in. I relayed my impression to Maximus.

He dipped his head. "Your impression is correct, Sam."

I next had an impression of the Asian philosophical yin and yang symbol, the white and black teardrop interconnected, and I understood that Archibald Maximus, and others like him, were here to balance a darkness that had taken root.

He said, "Do you understand, Samantha?"

"I think so, yes, but—"

"Good, good. Now, the medallions were created

for specific purposes."

I blinked, got the hint. He didn't want to talk about it. At least, not now. I said, "And why's that?"

"The reason, Samantha, is hidden even from me."

"But why?"

"The same reason why all the secrets of the universe are hidden from all humans, Samantha. Life on earth is our chance to grow, to learn, to observe, to interact, to trust, to give and to receive." He smiled sweetly at me. For someone who was centuries old, he was sure a cute little bugger. He said, "Now, much of what I just described would not be possible if we had all the answers."

"So, you're as much in the dark as me."

Now he gave me a slightly crooked smile. "Well, perhaps a little more in the light, Sam. Remember, I've been at this a lot longer than you."

"And you are an immortal, too?"

"In my own way."

"And what way is that?"

"One does not need to be a vampire, Samantha, or even a werewolf to be immortal."

In that moment, I saw a man working feverishly in an old-style laboratory. Something Benjamin Franklin might have worked in. Or even Leonardo da Vinci. I saw many concoctions being attempted. Many concoctions being tossed out. And one concoction in particular that gave eternal life.

"Alchemy," I said, breathing the word.

He grinned again...and tapped the book again. "Shall we get back to your medallion, Sam?"

I nodded.

"Good," he said. "Because I've some very good news for you."

17.

After my meeting with Max—and after a mad dash through the parking lot—I was back in my minivan, gasping.

Now, as I sat there shaking violently, watching college students strolling past with their backpacks and cell phones and serious faces, I knew that I was losing my humanity.

I hate when that happens.

I sucked in air because sucking in air seemed to help me fight off the excruciating pain caused by the sun. I had to fight off the pain because I had to pick my kids up from school. But I couldn't get my hands to stop shaking. Couldn't get them to form around the key and insert it into the ignition.

So I breathed and shook and tried to calm down.

And as I sat there, I recalled Max's words spoken to me just a few minutes earlier: "I have some very good news for you, Samantha," he'd said. "The emerald medallion is reputed to reverse the effects of...the sun."

"What, exactly, does that mean?" I had asked, not daring to believe what I thought it might mean.

"Once you unlock the medallion, Samantha Moon, the sun will no longer have power over you."

But his words were just not sinking in. It was just too much to hope for. Too much to believe. "I...I don't understand."

He had reached across the counter and gently took my hand. "It means, Sam, that you will be able to live in daylight again."

"But...how?"

He smiled mischievously. A mischievous smile in this situation was, in fact, maddening. He said, "Unlocking the secret to the medallion is easy enough, Sam, for those of great faith."

"Great faith? What does that mean?"

"You will know what to do, Sam."

Except I didn't know what to do. And, hell, when did I ever know what to do?

Now, as I continued to shake and breathe and burn in my van, I whispered his words again: "To live in daylight again."

I nearly wept at the thought.

Nearly. After all, I had my kids to pick up, and I wasn't going to be late again, dammit.

So, when the shaking had subsided enough to control the smaller movements of my fingers, I started the minivan, and as I drove, I saw myself at the beach with my kids, swimming with my kids, hiking with my kids. And watching my son play soccer in the bleachers with all the other parents.

Okay, now the tears found me.

And in my mind's eye, I saw myself sitting quietly high upon a faraway mountain and watching the sun rise for the first time in nearly seven years.

At the next red light, I buried my face in my hands and wept until the light turned green.

***

Damn.

I was a little late picking up the kids, which netted me a scowling look from the principal, whom I'm sure didn't like me much. I knew he saw me as an unfit mother, especially after the bogus ideas Danny had planted last year.

Bastard.

Bogus or not, I was now on the principal's radar. I hate being on anyone's radar, let alone a principal's. Sigh.

On the way home, we stopped for some burgers at Burger King. Anthony had branched out a little and discovered that he now liked mayonnaise. But just a little mayonnaise. My little boy was growing up.

At home, while the kids ate and I made yet another excuse for why I wasn't hungry, I found myself in my office and working when my cell phone rang. I glanced at the faceplate, saw that it was a local number.

"Moon Investigations," I said cheerily enough, although I was hearing the grumblings of a fight brewing in the living room.

"Ms. Moon?" said an oddly familiar voice.

"Go for Moon," I said. I've always wanted to say that.

"Ms. Moon, my name's Robert Mason. I own the Fullerton Playhouse."

"And starred in *One Life to Live*."

"I wouldn't say 'starred,' but, yes, I had a recurring role until a few years ago."

"When they killed you off with a brain tumor."

"It saddens the heart. Were you a fan?"

"It happened to come on after *Judge Judy*."

He laughed a little. A deep, rich laugh. A deep, rich, fake laugh. "*Judge Judy* was a great lead-in."

It was at that moment that a full-fledged fight broke out in the next room. I even heard something break. Something glass. Shit.

"Hang on, Rob," I said.

I left the phone on the desk, dashed into the living room and saw Anthony sitting on Tammy. Now that was a first. Tammy was always the bigger and stronger one. Granted, she was still bigger, but clearly not stronger. Her struggling seemed to be in vain. Indeed, she was looking at her brother oddly. No doubt marveling at what I was seeing, too.

I plucked him off his sister and deposited him on the new couch. I spent the next thirty-three seconds listening to "He said and she said and did that she started," and decided I'd heard enough. I turned the TV off and banished them both to their bedrooms. As they moped off, I couldn't help but notice the red mark around Tammy's arms where Anthony had pinned her to the floor.

Jesus.

Back in my office, I wasn't very surprised that Robert Mason hadn't hung up. After all, I suspected there was a very good reason why Robert Mason had called me.

After I apologized for the disruption, he said that was quite all right and that he wanted to meet me ASAP.

Yeah, that was the reason.

18.

I was waiting at Starbucks.

It was evening and the sun still had not set. By my internal vampire clock, I knew it was about twenty minutes away. My internal vampire clock also told me that I should be asleep, to awaken just as the sun set. I think, maybe, that's happened only two or three times. And that was when the whole family was sick.

Now, of course, only I was sick. Eternally sick.

The Starbucks was near the junior college, which meant there were a lot of young people inside with longish hair, random tattoos, squarish glasses, fuzzy beards, and cut-off jean shorts, all working importantly on their laptops. These were hipsters feeding and drinking in their natural habitat.

As I sat with my bottle of water, keenly aware that the two young men sitting at the table next to me were not only barefoot but one of them had tattoos of sandals on his feet, a handsome older gentleman stepped through the door, blinked, and scanned the coffee shop.

I waved. He spotted me and nodded. I think my stomach might have done a backflip. Someone might have gasped. Actually, that someone was me, never mind. The closer he got, the bluer his eyes got and the deeper the cleft in his chin seemed to get, too.

Not to mention, the darker his aura got.

I'm familiar with dark auras. The aura of the fallen angel who had visited me last Christmas had progressively gotten darker. Robert Mason's aura wasn't quite as foul, but the thick black cords that wove around and through him were disconcerting at best. What it meant, I didn't really know, but it couldn't be good.

Especially since my inner alarm began ringing.

He stood over me and reached out a hand, but now my warning bells were ringing so damn loud that I automatically recoiled. Women stared. Men stared. Hipsters glanced ironically. It was surely an odd scene. A renowned soap actor and a skittish woman afraid to make contact with him.

After another second or two, he retracted his hand and sat without me saying a word. As he made himself comfortable, I noted that the black snakes now moved over and under the table, slithering like living things. I shivered. No, *shuddered.*

He watched me closely. "Some would be insulted that you didn't shake my hand."

"And you?" I asked, noting that my voice sounded higher than normal. I verified the mental wall around my thoughts was impenetrable.

He tilted his head slightly, studying me. "I find it curious. You seem to be having a sort of...reaction to my presence. Why is that?"

"Well, you are the great Robert Mason, famous for playing the evil Dr. Conch on *One Life To Live*."

He continued studying me as he adjusted the drape of his slacks. He was, I noted, the only man in Starbucks wearing slacks. Maybe the only man ever. His jawline, I noticed, was impossibly straight. The women all checked him out, but he paid them no mind. Indeed, he only looked at me. No, stared at me. So intently that he was giving me the willies.

After a moment, he said, "Or perhaps you didn't want me to touch you, Ms. Moon. Is there something about me that repels you?"

"Your jawline," I said.

"What about my jawline?"

"It's impossibly straight."

His right hand, which was laying flat on the smooth table, twitched slightly. The black snakes that wove through his aura seemed to pick up their pace a little. The jawline in question rippled a little as he unconsciously bit down. He said, "I think you see things, Ms. Moon. Perhaps things around me. Tell me what you see."

"I thought we were here to discuss Brian Meeks."

His lips thinned into a weak smile. "Of course, Ms. Moon. What would you like to ask?"

Except that before I could open my mouth to speak, I felt something push against my mind, against the protective mental wall, and it kept on pushing, searching, feeling.

It was Robert Mason, who was staring at me intently. The man was extremely psychic.

My thoughts were not closed to those who were psychic. Only to other immortals and often to my own family members. Someone like Robert Mason could gain entry...if I wasn't vigilant.

I knew this wasn't really a meeting, but a feeling out of sorts. He wanted to know who he was up against. By not gaining entry into my thoughts, he might have gotten his answer. What that answer was, or how close to the truth he got, I didn't know.

So, I decided to ask him the only question that mattered. "Did you kill Brian Meeks?"

The coiling, smoky black snakes that wove in and out of his aura seemed to pick up in intensity. They appeared and disappeared. Robert Mason didn't react to my question. He sat calmly, hands resting on the table, blue eyes shining. Although I think the dimple in his chin might have quivered a little.

After a moment, he said, "Ah, but that wouldn't be any fun, would it? Taking away all the mystery?"

His own thoughts, of course, were closed to me, which I was eternally thankful for. I was honestly afraid to know what was lurking inside that handsome head of his. Hard to believe that one of America's favorite daytime soap opera stars was so damn...creepy.

"There's a door in the prop room," I said. "A door behind the big mirror. Where does it lead to?"

I probably shouldn't have asked him about the door. I probably should have left well enough alone and directed Sherbet to the door later. But I wanted to see Robert Mason's reaction now, and I got the one I was looking for. His eyes widened briefly, just enough for me to know that I was onto something.

He said, "How do you know about the door, Ms. Moon?"

"We all have our secrets. And taking away the mystery wouldn't be any fun, right?"

He looked at me. I looked at him. We did this for a few seconds, then he said. "I suppose. Very well, Ms. Moon. The door leads to another prop room. A long-forgotten prop room."

"Why did you call this meeting?"

"I saw you in the theater the other day. You looked interesting."

"Interesting how?"

He suddenly leaned over the small, wobbly table and whispered, "I know what you are, Ms. Moon. Mystery solved."

And with that, he got up, winked at me, and walked out.

19.

We were in Tammy's bedroom.

She was sitting on the floor in front of me while I brushed her long, dark hair. Tammy loved having her hair brushed, even when my cold fingers sometimes grazed her neck, inadvertently causing her to shudder. She used to hold my hands, back in the days when my hands were warm. These days, however, she almost never held my hands, and I didn't blame her. Who'd want to hold hands with a living corpse?

I cherished these quiet moments when I brushed her hair, listening to her stories about school and boys, teachers and boys, and movies and boys. She often asked me what it was like to kiss a boy or to be in love. She sometimes asked why Daddy and I were no longer together. Mostly we laughed and giggled, and if we were being too loud, Anthony would sometimes stick his head in the door and tell us we were being lame.

Tonight, Anthony was in the living room watching cartoons. Something on Nick at Night. He laughed, slapping his hand on the carpet the way he does when he sits on the floor. The vibration reached even us.

"Cartoons are so juvenile," said Tammy.

"Totally," I said.

"I haven't watched them in, like, a year."

"Same here."

"Well, I guess there are one or two that are okay, but mostly they're lame."

"Mostly," I said, nodding.

Anthony erupted in laughter again, hitting the floor even harder. The thuds reverberated up through our butts.

"God, he's so annoying," said Tammy. She didn't sound annoyed. She sounded impressed that she knew the word "annoying."

"He's eight years old," I said, as if that explained everything.

She shrugged and I continued brushing her long hair. Warm air from the heater vent washed over us. The TV blared from the living room. I cherished these small moments.

"Mommy?"

"Yes, baby?"

"There's something different about Anthony."

I stopped brushing. I think my heart might have stopped altogether. I resumed brushing and kept my voice as calm as possible. "Different how?" I asked.

"Well, yesterday I saw him wrestling with some other boys."

"Boys like to wrestle. It's what makes them boys."

"No, not that. He was wrestling the other boys."

"What do you mean, honey?"

She turned and looked back at me, her big round eyes looking at me like I was the world's biggest dolt. And maybe I was. "It was him against like seven other boys."

"They ganged up on him? That's not fair—"

"No, Mommy. They didn't gang up on him. They couldn't do anything to him. He was throwing them around like they were, you know..."

"Rag dolls?"

"What's a rag doll?"

"Never mind."

She went on to tell me that Anthony Moon, aged eight, was probably the strongest kid in their school.

I processed that information as I continued to brush. Somehow the subject turned to zits and I was telling her about the big one I got on my right nostril when I was in the tenth grade, and soon Tammy was doubled over on her side with laughter. From in the next room, I was vaguely aware of the TV being turned off and the trudging of footsteps.

Anthony stuck his head in his sister's room, looked at us on the floor and said, "Lame."

And walked on.

20.

Hi, Moon Dance.

Hey, big guy.

Big guy?

It's a term of affection, I wrote.

So you feel affection for me?

Of course I do, Fang.

I felt him probing my mind a little, small, shivery touches that let me know he was there.

He wrote: *I think you love me, Moon Dance.*

Friendly love, Fang.

I'll take friendly love. For now.

Good. Now, what's up?

I've got news about your son.

Talk to me.

First of all, is he still becoming stronger?

More so than ever. Tammy said he now routinely wrestles seven boys at once.

So, you could say he's seven times stronger.

Put that way, and I nearly went into a panic. I wrote: *Yes, I guess. What does it mean?*

I can feel you panicking, Moon Dance. Don't panic.

Please just tell me what's going on, Fang. I can't handle this. I'm seriously freaking out.

Okay, okay, hang in there. According to my sources, the vampire blood that briefly flowed through him hasn't entirely left him.

"Oh my God," I said out loud to the empty room. More panic gripped me. Nearly overwhelmed me. I wrote: *But the vampirism has been reversed, Fang. The medallion...*

Yes, the vampirism has been reversed. No, your son isn't a vampire. Not technically.

I found myself on my feet, reeling, staggering, pacing. Jesus, what had I done to my son?

The IM window pinged with a new message. I sat back down. Fang had written: *Hang on, Moon Dance. It's not all bad. In fact, it's kind of good news, if you ask me.*

Kind of? What the hell is going on, Fang? Please tell me.

Sam, your son will have all the strength of a vampire, but none of the weaknesses.

I read his words, blinking through tears. *Are you sure?*

Pretty sure.

He won't need to consume blood?

We don't think so.

Who's we?

My sources.

Fine, I wrote. I didn't care about Fang's sources. Not now. I wrote: *What about the sunlight?*

It should not affect him, Moon Dance.

And immortality?

There was a small delay, followed by: *Perhaps.*

Perhaps what?

There's a good chance your son might be immortal.

I don't understand. Why?

I don't think anyone really understands, Sam. The system was flawed somewhere, broke down. But, yes, we think he will retain the good qualities but none of the bad.

And being immortal is a good quality?

For some, the very best, Moon Dance.

But why did this happen?

Whoever created your kind, and whoever created the medallion, was not perfect. In essence, a mistake was made somewhere along the line. The reverse was not complete.

What do I do, Fang?

It is up to you to make the most of this, Moon Dance, and to help your son make the most of this, too. Think of this as an opportunity, Moon Dance. Not a curse. For both you and your son.

I hung my head for a minute or two, then typed: *Thanks for your help, Fang.*

So what will you do, Moon Dance?

I'm going to have a talk with him.

When?
I don't know. Goodnight, Fang.
Goodnight, Moon Dance.

21.

Celebrities can hide their electronic footprints a little easier than the average citizen. This is because they can hide behind accountants and handlers. Because of this, my background search on Robert Mason took a little more digging than usual.

And what came up wasn't much.

I had his current residence. Or, rather, his last known residence. He was living in the hills above Fullerton. Nice area. Big homes. Lots of space. Perfect place to secretly drain someone dry. Or maybe many someones.

Interestingly, I knew of two people who also lived in the hills. Detective Hanner and a very old and very creepy Kabbalistic grandmaster. One was a vampire, and one was a kind of vampire.

Anyway, Robert Mason had no criminal record. An ex-wife of his accused him of abuse. He was never arrested, although a restraining order had been placed on him. I'd only met the guy once, and I wanted to put a restraining order on him, too. He had no kids, only the one marriage—divorced now fifteen years.

His last known professional acting job had been on *One Life to Live*, five years ago. And, according to the various reports I'd dug up, he'd been fired from his job. The reasons were conflicting, but more than one article suggested substance abuse.

Why he was fired or why he was divorced didn't seem to be of importance presently. That he was a full-blown psychopath now was obvious to me. That he harbored a deep evil was also obvious to me.

As I sat in my office, with my kids asleep down the hallway, I called Kingsley. He picked up on the second ring.

"Hi, baby," he said.

I didn't respond. At least, not with words.

"What's that sound?" he asked.

"I'm panting," I said. "You know, like a dog."

"Oh, brother. But, please, Sam. Say no more over the phone."

"Oh, I'm not saying anything," I said, and panted some more.

"Cute, Sam. Do you actually have something on your mind, or did you just call to make those ridiculous sounds?"

"Both," I said, and stopped panting long enough to catch him up to date on my investigation—in particular, my meeting with Robert Mason.

"Like he said," said Kingsley. "He knows what you are, Sam."

"In so short a time?"

"He must have suspected you were something more, which is why he scheduled the meeting. No doubt his suspicions were confirmed at the meeting." Kingsley paused. I knew he was choosing his words carefully over the open phone line. "We can hide from the majority of the world, Sam, but not from the truly psychic. They tend to see through us. Thankfully, there's not many of them."

"And those who do see us?"

"Well, those who are vocal about it are silenced."

I thought about his words. "I think Robert Mason saw an opportunity."

"To supply blood?"

"Yes," I said.

"No doubt a very lucrative gig."

I asked, "What do you know about blood suppliers?"

"Not much, but I know someone who undoubtedly would."

"Detective Hanner," I said.

"Boy, Sam. It's almost as if you could read my mind."

"I'll never say."

He laughed and we set up a dinner date later in the week, and when we had hung up, I made another call.

To the only other creature of the night that I knew.

22.

We were on her wide, wraparound patio deck.

The deck overlooked the same Fullerton Hills that Robert Mason lived in. And a famous Dodgers manager. And a very creepy old man who bartered in human life.

Detective Hanner was a beautiful woman. She was also a vampire. Perhaps a very old vampire.

We talked a little about the case as we sat back in wicker chairs, drinking from glasses just like regular people. My ankles were crossed and my pink New Balance running shoes couldn't have looked cuter. Detective Hanner was barefoot. Her talon-like toenails came to sharp points. Almost enough for one to lose one's appetite.

Almost.

But not quite. After all, we were both drinking from massive goblets of blood. We were sipping casually. Or trying to sip casually. Generally, there were long beats of silence as we each glugged heartily, since drinking blood is really a race against time and coagulation. It was all I could do to not make yummy smacking sounds. The blood was human, that much was obvious. It was also fresh. So very, very fresh.

Straight-from-the-vein fresh.

So who am I drinking? I wondered.

But I didn't ask. Not at the moment. At the moment, I was consumed by the blood, the taste, the high, the joy, the pleasure, the satisfaction.

Detective Hanner and Kingsley had slowly introduced me to the decadent pleasure of human blood. I hadn't liked it, not at first, and each time felt like a depraved journey into ecstasy.

That's a lie. You always liked it. A little too much.

And here I was again, indulging all my cravings with a vampire far older and more experienced than I was. It felt natural, probably the way any addict feels when they tap the needle or pop a cork. Like this was what I was made to do.

But I didn't have to enjoy its thick, sweet texture so much, did I?

Finally, I managed to pull away. I knew some blood was running down the corners of my mouth. Now, as I wiped my chin and licked my fingers, I could only imagine what I looked like.

Like a monster, I thought.

Hanner watched me from over her own goblet, her wild eyes shining with supernatural intensity. I noticed that she rarely blinked, and when she did, it almost seemed an afterthought. A reminder to look human.

I said, "I think our killer is a blood supplier."

She nodded. "It's easy to assume that."

"What do you know of blood suppliers?"

"Mortal or immortal?"

"What do you mean?" I asked.

"Vampires supply blood to other vampires. Like I just did you."

"Mortal," I said.

She held my gaze for many seconds. I couldn't read her mind, or even get a feel for what she was thinking, but I suspected she was debating how much to tell me. Finally, she said, "Yes, some are killers, although many get their supply from hospitals or mortuaries."

"Mortuaries?"

She nodded. "Of course. Why let all that valuable blood drain away when it could be put to good use?" She held up her nearly-finished goblet. "But fresh human blood is always preferable."

"How fresh?"

"Straight from a living source, even if that living source dies shortly thereafter."

I shuddered. Even though I knew most of this already, it always chilled me to think about it. And a cold-blooded vampire like me is hard to chill. "Why a living source?"

"Because blood is suffused with life force, Sam. Energies that vibrate at the cellular level. The residual energy left behind in animal blood—or that from a human corpse that's been deceased for an extended period—doesn't vibrate at the same frequency. Such blood is not in tune with who you are, Sam."

"So the fresher the blood..."

"The stronger we are. The healthier we are. The more extraordinary we are."

"How many mortal blood dealers are there?"

"Not many."

"Do you know of any?"

She stared at me for an uncomfortable amount of time. "I have found having a living donor in my house to be more ideal. A ready source, as they say." She grinned. "Sometimes, many ready sources."

I wondered if she used her looks to lure her living donors. Some guys would do anything to be with a woman as beautiful as her. Anything.

As we sat back in the wicker chairs, aglow with fresh blood, I realized that Detective Hanner hadn't really answered my question.

Now, why was that?

23.

My alarm clock blared.

It did this for a full five minutes before I emerged from whatever black abyss I descend into when asleep. Another five minutes before I could move my legs enough to sit up in bed. Truly, I was the waking dead.

As I sat there on the edge of the bed, wishing like hell I was back in that abyss, my cell phone chimed with a text message. I flopped my hand onto night stand, felt around until I found my phone, brought it over to my half-open eyes.

A text from Danny, my dear old ex-husband, only not so dear anymore. It was simple and to the point and aggravated me to no end: *Coming over. Need help.*

"Shit."

And just as I deleted his message—as I do all his messages—there was a loud knocking sound on the front door.

"Shit," I said again. Definitely not how I wanted to start my day.

Ever.

I hauled my ass out of bed, stumbled through my room, then plodded barefoot to the front door. Along the way, I grabbed my sunglasses from the kitchen table, put them on, and opened the front door.

It was, of course, Danny. In all his pitiful glory, silhouetted against the glare from the afternoon sunlight. Too much sunlight, especially after just awakening. I backed up, shielding my eyes, feeling like something out of a Bela Lugosi movie.

"Sam, can we talk?"

"Do I have a choice?"

He came in, shutting the door quickly. Danny knew the routine. He'd lived long enough with my condition to know what to do. I felt my way over to the dining room chair and sank down.

"Geez, Sam. You don't look too well."

"Ya think."

Now that he was inside, I took in his unshaven face, wrinkled suit, disheveled hair, and couldn't find the energy to say something about the pot calling the kettle black. Instead, I said, "What do you want, Danny?"

"I need to hire you, Sam."

I nearly laughed. Hell, I wanted to laugh. Except laughing was for people who hadn't just emerged from the blackest depths. "You're kidding."

"I'm serious, Sam. I need to hire you."

"You, who hasn't paid me a dime of child support in seven months?"

He shifted in his seat. As he did so, I saw that his upper lip was swollen. "I know, Sam, and I'm sorry. This hasn't been easy on me, either."

I didn't want to get into it with Danny. At least not now. Hell, I had a whole lifetime to get into it with him.

"Fine," I said. "What kind of help?"

"Protection."

"What kind of protection?"

"From men."

"What kind of men?"

He looked away, adjusted his tie, giving his Adam's apple more wiggle room. "They're a gang, of sorts."

"Of sorts? What does that mean?"

Now I saw the sweat on his brow and along his upper lip. I also saw the fear in his eye. He waved his hands weakly. "Thugs. A local street gang, I dunno. They sort of run the area I do business in."

"They beat you up?"

He shrugged, too prideful to admit to being smacked around, but not enough to come to his ex-wife for help.

I said, "And by doing business, you mean that shithole where you charge lonely men to look at lonelier women's boobs?"

"Yes, Sam. My strip club."

I shook my head sadly.

"What, Sam?"

"You used to be ashamed of your club."

He was pacing now, running his hand through his thinning hair. "Well, I'm too afraid to be ashamed."

"Sit down," I said. "You're making me nervous."

He sat, although his knee still bounced up and down. I said, "They're extorting money from you."

He nodded. "A grand a week. For protection, of course."

"Of course," I said. "So what do you want me to do?"

He frowned a little. He hadn't really thought this through. "I'm not sure."

"Do you want them to stop picking on you?"

"Sam..."

"What?"

"Fine. Yes."

"The price for keeping these boys from picking on you is..." I did some quick math, which, in my groggy state, took a little longer than it should have. I said, "The price is four thousand, two hundred and sixty-two dollars."

"Jesus, Sam. You can't be serious."

"Oh, but I am. Seven months of child support, plus my usual fee. Have the cash here on my table in one hour and you just hired yourself a bodyguard."

He looked down at his hands. His knee continued to bounce. Loose change in his pocket clanged. Finally, he nodded and stood.

"I'll be back," he said.

"We'll see."

He did come back. Funny what a little fear will do to a man. He handed me a white envelope full of money, which I counted in front of him. Once done, I grinned and held out my hand. He looked at it reluctantly, then finally shook it, wincing as he did so.

After all, I might have squeezed a little too hard.

24.

I was sitting cross-legged on a large boulder, on a rock-strewn hill, high above the deserts outside Corona.

I was, in fact, not too far from where Brian Meeks had been found. Or dumped. It was a quiet spot, miles from any major roads. Just me, the lizards, and the coyotes. And maybe a rattlesnake or two.

In the far distance I could hear the steady drone of the 15 Freeway. In the near distance, all I could hear was the wind, moaning gently over the boulder and, subsequently, me. Rocking me a little. I let the wind rock me, as I felt the latent heat from the boulder rise up through my jeans.

My minivan was parked on a dirt service road not too far from here. The service road had been closed off by a locked gate. Amazingly, the lock just happened to fall apart in my hands as I innocently examined it. Shoddy workmanship.

So, what the hell, I let myself in.

Now my jeans were dusty and my cute shoes were officially dirty. But I didn't care. I needed to be out here. Craving the solace, the peace, the oneness.

I closed my eyes and rested my hands on my knees. My children were at home with the sitter, and so I let all worry for them disappear. I took a deep breath, not because I needed the oxygen, but because I wanted to center myself. Years ago, I had done yoga. I knew something about centering myself.

Months ago, I had learned the art of automatic writing, in which one channels another entity to receive messages from angels, or the spirit world, or from Jim Morrison.

Either way, the results were interesting, but now I was determined to go beyond automatic writing. To go deeper, straight to the source. And what was the source? I didn't know. Not entirely. But I was determined to find out.

With my eyes still shut, I tilted my face up toward the heavens, and was met immediately by a mostly cool breeze laced with some tendrils of heat. I always welcomed heat, no matter how small or fleeting.

I focused on my breathing, releasing my thoughts to the wind, where I imagined them being snatched up and escorted far away. To meditate—to do it right—I had to have my mind blank. As blank as I could make it.

Breathing was the key. No, the act of focusing on my breathing was the key. Focusing on something simple. Mindless. It settles the mind. Relaxes it. Bypasses the ego. The ego, the fore-mind, that thing with which we use to calculate and imagine and worry and ponder, didn't like to be bypassed. The ego liked to remain in control.

So I continued concentrating on the fresh air flowing into my lungs. Despite my best efforts, my mind drifted to my son and soon worry gripped me, but I released that thought, too. To the wind.

Breathing.

Flowing in and out.

In and out.

Over lips and teeth and tongue...deep into my lungs.

I thought of blood dealers and corpses hanging upside down.

I shivered and released that thought, too. Into the wind.

My mind felt blank, although fleeting images sometimes crossed it. Kingsley. Fang. Sherbet. Strong men. Strange men. Sexy men.

I released those thoughts, too.

I felt myself relaxing as I did more deep breathing. I didn't need to breathe, granted, but oxygen in this case wasn't the purpose here. The purpose here was to relax my mind. To calm it. To calm it so completely that I could access...what?

I didn't know.

But I was about to find out.

Breathe in, breathe out.

Breathe in, Samantha.

Just breathe.

It's easy. Yes, so easy. Do you see how easy it is, Sam? Focus, child. There now. Good, good. Just focus on your breathing. You're almost there. Good, good.

Good...

It took a moment for me to realize that the thoughts in my head were no longer my own.

Welcome back, Samantha Moon, said the voice.

25.

I knew I was still sitting on the boulder overlooking the desert, but I also knew that something very, very strange was happening to me.

The strangeness boiled down to a feeling. I felt unhinged, disconnected from my body. I knew I was sitting cross-legged on the hard surface, but I felt as if I were somewhere else, too. Not necessarily above my body. Somewhere else. Where, exactly, I didn't know. As I thought about this, I suddenly felt a jolting wave of dizziness.

Ground yourself, Sam, said the voice.

I knew something about grounding, having done it back when I was doing the automatic writing. Quickly, I imagined three silver ropes, attached to my ankles and lower spine, reaching all the way down into the earth—down, down—all the way to the center of the earth, where they fastened themselves around three massive boulders.

Grounded. To the very earth itself.

Very good, Sam.

Instantly, the feeling of separateness ceased. I was back in my body. Although my eyes were still closed, I began seeing light appear at the peripherals of my vision. The light continued filling my head, growing steadily brighter, so bright that I was suddenly sure it wasn't coming from inside my mind after all. Surely it was coming from somewhere beyond me. Above me. Around me. Within me. From everywhere.

And from within that light I saw a vague shape materialize. A woman. A glowing woman. Her face and body remained indistinct.

Baby steps, Samantha. I'll reveal more later. Once you've gotten the hang of this.

Hang of what?

Speaking to me.

Who are you?

Everything and nothing.

I don't understand.

You will. In time.

The light coalesced into a room made of crystal. Now the burning white light shone brightly beyond, refracting through the crystal, exploding, washing over me. For the first time in a long, long time, I didn't shrink from the light.

Where am I?

The woman stepped closer to me. She was, in fact, a lovely older woman. Roundish. Happy, smiling face. Pink cheeks. She looked like anyone's kind grandmother. Serenity surrounded her, radiated from her.

You are in a safe place, Samantha.

What's happening to me?

You've bypassed the physical world and entered into the spiritual.

But I'm still sitting here on the ledge.

Yes, Sam. The spiritual is never very far away. In fact, it's closer than most people think.

I don't understand.

You will. In time.

You keep saying that.

Because it keeps being true.

So I'm in the physical, but also in the spiritual? I'm in both places?

You are more than your physical body, Sam. The body is the physical receptacle of the soul.

Except my body can't die.

Not anymore. Not in the traditional sense.

Then I'm a freak.

You are the result of entities long ago attempting a shortcut, entities who lived in fear.

Lived in fear of what?

Dying. Their creation—the vampire—lives on to this day, as do similar creations.

I never asked for this.

Not overtly, Sam.

What does that mean?

It means that, on some level, you did *ask for this. On some level you* did *ask to become more than you were, stronger than you were, faster than you were, braver than you were.*

And this is the answer? To turn me into a ghoul?

It was an *answer. An answer that you would accept.*

But I'm living a nightmare.

You are choosing to live a nightmare, Samantha Moon. Choose differently.

I grew silent, fully aware that I was still sitting on the boulder overlooking the desert, but also aware that my mind—or spirit—was in this crystal room. I'm certain the sensation would have disoriented me, if not for the grounding done earlier. The woman moved a little closer, her hands clasped before her. She seemed content to watch me sweetly, lovingly.

Who are you? I asked, thinking the words. *And please, no cryptic answers.*

Now the woman in front of me disappeared. So did the crystal room. I was given a view of the universe, which spread before me in every direction. I sensed everything, saw everything, felt everything. I also sensed a glorious presence that infused everything, a presence from which all things were born.

Is that you? The thing that which is in all things? Everywhere and nowhere?

A good way of looking at things, Sam.

But, then, why are you talking to me?

As I thought those words, I was once again back in the crystal room. I sensed that if I would open my physical eyes, all of this would disappear and I would be back on the boulder, alone in the desert, and no doubt wondering if I had dreamed all of this. So, I kept my eyes closed. Yes, tightly closed.

Because you are seeking answers, child. I have the answers.

To everything?

In a word: Yes.

I let that sink in. Beyond the crystal walls, the shining white light seemed to grow in intensity, its radiance reaching through the walls and through me, too. My body felt cleansed. My body felt light. There was no judgment in this light. It just was. Pure and perfect and eternal.

The smiling woman before me cocked her head to one side. *You are here for a specific reason, Sam.*

I am.

Tell me what's on your heart.

I thought of my son, of his increasing strength. What would happen to him? What other vampiric attributes would he take on? I thought of this and more, as fear and uncertainly coursed through me. As these thoughts filled my head, the light wavered along the peripheral of my vision. The woman in front of me faded, too. She nodded, and I knew she knew my thoughts.

Release the fear, Sam.

But I...can't. He's my son. I'm so scared.

More darkness encroached and the light beyond dimmed.

She gripped my hands even tighter. *What do you want, Sam?*

I want my son to have a normal life.

Then proclaim it. State it. Feel it. Believe it. Do not grovel for it. Do not beg for it. Instead...be it.

But something's happening to him.

Yes.

Something that I did to him.

She nodded and held my hands, and for now, the darkness that had been encroaching along the edge of my vision seemed to pause, although it was still there. Seemingly waiting.

Find the good in all things, Sam. Find the beauty. And you will find peace and joy.

But my son...he's so different now.

We are all different, Sam. And we are all the same. Love who he is. Teach him who he is. Believe in who he is.

And who is he?

A magnificent being, as are you.

I held back the tears. I held back a strong urge to let out a choking cry. It had been so long since someone had spoken to me in such kind, loving words. Since someone had given me such pure, unconditional love.

But will he be okay?

With his mother's love, he can be anything. Show him love and strength, Sam. Not fear and worry.

I nodded. The darkness began retreating, and as I lifted my head and opened my heart, the darkness disappeared completely. The woman came toward me and took my hands. She smiled at me comfortingly and lovingly.

Open your eyes now, Sam.

I did, and I was back on the boulder, with the wind blowing in my hair and dust covering my clothes. I sat like that for a few moments, coming back to my senses, back to my body. Shortly, I checked my cell. I had been sitting there for three hours. I stared disbelievingly at my phone. Three hours. It had felt like ten minutes.

Something squeezed my hands, something unseen, and electricity surged through me. No, not electricity.

Love.

The feeling rippled through me again and again, then slowly disappeared, and I was left alone.

26.

It was late.

I was perched on the ridge of a high gable next door to Robert's Mason's opulent home. Granted, the home I was perched upon wasn't too shabby, either. The entire tract was filled with mini-mansions, all nestled in the hills high above Fullerton. The community was gated. In fact, there were even two sets of gates. Twice I spotted security guards rolling quietly through the streets in their electric golf carts. Never once did they think to look up at me. If so, they might have been in for the shock of their lives.

I had spent the past two days reviewing missing-person files with Sherbet. In particular, looking for a connection to Robert Mason. Sherbet knew about my strange meeting with the ex-soap opera star. The detective agreed that if we could connect another victim to Robert Mason, then we might convince a judge to give us a search warrant.

But so far, nothing.

This was my second night of surveillance, too. Or, more accurately, my second night perched up here like a living gargoyle. The first night had been uneventful. Robert Mason had come home around 2 a.m., pulling into his garage in a slick new Jaguar. His windows were tinted, too dark for even my eyes. The lights had remained on inside the house for about an hour after that, in which I'd seen only one figure moving through the house. I had waited another two hours, then leaped from the perch, flapped my wings hard, and somehow managed to elude the two guards in their electric golf cart.

Now I was back for a second night. What, exactly, was I looking for? I didn't know. A pattern perhaps. Something that stood out. Who he was meeting with. Who was coming and going? Anything that I could follow up on.

Tonight, the house was empty and dark. It was also well past the time he'd returned last night. Instinctively, I knew the sun was about two hours away, about the time I had abandoned my post last night.

So, where was Robert Mason?

I knew he lived alone. I knew he was divorced. I knew his ex-wife had a restraining order on him. I also knew that everything was leading to one thing: the secret door behind the mirror.

So far, his house was proving uneventful, although I now knew the freaky bastard was prone to staying out all night. Whatever was happening, it wasn't happening here, in this ultra-exclusive and highly-secured community. Poke fun at them all I want, the guards here kept strict schedules. Nothing much was coming or going without their knowledge. If Robert Mason was the killer, he was taking a phenomenal risk bringing any victims here.

Unlike his theater.

Which he owned and had total access to at all hours of the night.

The golf cart came again. Two guards, sitting next to each other, huddled against the cold. I didn't huddle against the cold. I sat like a demon, high above the housing tract.

Waiting and watching.

27.

I parked across the street from my ex-husband's strip club. Remarkably, a tear of shattered pride did not come to my eye.

Danny and his partners of sleazeballs had cleaned up the place a little. The ugly cinder block building had been painted white. The dirt parking lot had been paved over. And a flashing neon sign now indicated that here be nude women. I shook my head sadly. Men slouched in and out of the club. Single men. Most didn't appear happy. A big black guy stood at the front entrance checking ID's. Music pumped enthusiastically from the open door.

I sat and watched, my heart heavy. Above, the moon was half-full. The stars were out. No clouds. No wind. A perfect night to see desperate women exploited for dollar bills.

I was feeling sick, and not because I was parked outside Danny's house of flesh. Earlier, I had consumed a packet of animal blood. Pig blood, this time. The impurities in the blood always made me sick. My digestive system was designed for blood only. Not the bits of bone, hair and meat floating around in the stuff they sold me. I probably should filter the blood myself, but I honestly didn't want to see what I was drinking. Better to tear the packet open, close my eyes, down the stuff as fast as possible, and will myself not to gag.

Impurities or not, the animal blood never truly revitalized me. It satisfied a hunger, a craving. It kept me alive and functioning. But it did not energize me. Not the way human blood did. And that scared the shit out of me.

There was really no comparison. My kind was obviously designed to consume human blood. And there was such a ready supply of the stuff.

Mercifully, the animal blood kept my hunger in check, but I wondered for how long. Would there come a day when animal blood would no longer suffice? I didn't know, but that thought alone was enough get me rocking in my front seat, holding my aching stomach.

A few minutes later, with my stomach still doing somersaults, I pulled away from the curb, drove past the strip club, and was soon trawling through some pretty rough-looking neighborhoods. Most homes here were surrounded with low, wrought-iron fences. Most windows were barred. More wrought iron. Clearly, iron work was alive and well here in Colton.

Five minutes later, while waiting for a light at a mostly empty corner, I watched a boy on a bike ride up to three young men lounging near a liquor store. The boy gave a tall black guy an envelope. The black guy gave the boy a baggie.

Bingo.

I pulled up next to them in a no-parking zone. I parked there anyway and got out. They stared at me. I was wearing jeans and a light sweater. They were wearing jeans and heavy jackets. The heavy jackets reminded me of the Michelin Man, or maybe something astronauts might wear in deep space. This wasn't deep space. This was a hood in Colton and I knew what was inside their jackets. Drugs and guns. I had to act quickly.

"Hey pretty lady—" one of them said, turning to me.

But that was as far as he got. I punched him hard enough to lift him off his feet and into the liquor store wall behind him. While he was busy passing out, I turned and punched the lone Hispanic guy square in the nose. His head snapped back so violently that I thought I might have broken his neck. One moment he was standing there. The next, he was on his back and bleeding.

The third guy was making a move to reach inside his too-thick jacket when I slapped him hard enough to get his attention, but not so hard as to knock him out cold. A few encouraging smacks later, followed by a knee to the groin, and I had the information I was looking for.

Their boss was guy named Johnny. And he was here. At the liquor store.

I smacked the third guy again, this time for selling drugs to kids, and sent him spinning into my minivan's front fender, which he promptly bounced off of, leaving a skull-sized dent. He lay unmoving on the sidewalk.

Now, how the hell was I going to explain that to my insurance agent?

I headed into the liquor store.

28.

It was empty, except for an old black man sitting behind the counter. Apparently, he hadn't heard the ruckus outside. He was casually flipping through a newspaper, safe behind his bulletproof glass which sported two deep fractures. Bullet impacts.

I scanned the store. There was a back room, from which I heard voices. I headed toward it, passing a glass cooler and a Red Bull display along the way. The smell of weed grew steadily stronger as I approached the back door, which I promptly kicked in.

There were two of them, both smoking and drinking and playing cards. Rap music played in the background. The room was just big enough for the two goons to sit comfortably. On the far wall, an open door led down a short hallway. Two big handguns were sitting on the table. They reached for them. I did, too. Unfortunately for them, I was faster.

I pointed both weapons at them. "Don't move," I said.

They didn't move. I left the room and headed down the short hallway. There was a shut door at the far end. Yellow light under the door. I heard frantic shuffling inside.

I picked up my speed, and threw a shoulder into the door and spilled into the room, rolling, coming to my knees and holding both handguns out before me as the only man came up from behind his desk holding a shotgun.

He saw the weapons pointed at his face and made a very smart move. He set the weapon down on the desk and held his hands up. He was a handsome black man. Young, maybe twenty-five, maybe a little older. His teeth were perfect and he was wearing a nice suit. He looked, if anything, like a young man trying to be taken seriously. Trying to be something he wasn't.

"Sit down," I said.

He sat, watching me closely, curiously. Since there was nowhere for me to sit, I went around and sat on the corner of his desk, next to him. Our knees were almost touching. I heard some noise down the hallway, but I wasn't worried about the noise down the hall. My inner alarm was not ringing. There was no real danger here. At least, not yet. The smell of weed was not so prevalent in the back room.

"We have a problem, Johnny," I said.

"What problem?" he asked easily, smoothly, confidently.

Johnny didn't sound like a kid from the streets. He was well-spoken. Enunciated his words crisply. He also watched me carefully. No doubt his brain was having a hard time processing what he was seeing. A woman. A white woman. A lone white woman. Here in my office. I'm sure it wasn't adding up. No doubt it wasn't computing. And so he stared and waited and processed.

"You've been threatening local businesses," I said. "Extorting money from hard-working people."

His eyes narrowed. "You a cop?"

I swung my feet a little. My sneakers just missed hitting the ratty carpet. "Nope."

"You with the feds?"

I smiled. "Just little ol' me."

"Who are you?"

"Now, if I told you that I'd have to kill you."

He stared at me. I smiled sweetly. Sweat rolled down from inside his hairline and made its way into his collar. This wasn't looking good to him, and he knew it. In fact, I could almost see the moment where he went from thinking this was surreal, to thinking his own life might actually be in jeopardy.

"What do you want?"

"You're going to stop extorting from local business. Got it?"

He sat back in his chair and relaxed a little. He said, "You're kind of a badass, huh?"

"Kind of."

He was handsome and he knew it. He gave me a bright smile and did something with his eyes that made them sparkle even more somehow. As if he could flip a switch.

He chuckled. "You come in here, kick in my door, and tell me how to run my business."

"That about sums it up."

"You might be the craziest bitch I've ever met."

"Maybe."

"Now, why is that?"

"Let's just say I've got mad skills."

Now he laughed, a deep, hearty laugh, and showed a lot of teeth. Nice laugh. Nice smile.

"Mad skills," he said. "That's good. Who are you working for, baby?"

"An interested party. But I don't say 'goo goo gah gah' and I'm not wearing diapers, so I'm not a baby."

"Okay, I get it. Now, if I don't suspend operations?"

"You'll be seeing me again."

He held my gaze. I think I swallowed a little harder than I intended to.

"Maybe that ain't such a bad thing," he said.

"Just ask your boys outside."

He laughed again, shook his head. "You're one freaky lady. Okay, you win. No collections. For now."

"Smart move."

I got up, headed for the door. As I was about to exit, he said, "Can I have my guns back? I do, after all, have a business to run."

I paused at the door and thought about it, then turned and set the pistols next to the shotgun. I said, "I'm watching you."

His eyes flashed. "I hope so, pretty lady."

I turned and left.

29.

"Your son was in a fight today, Ms. Moon," said Principal West.

I was in his office with Anthony, who was sitting next to me. Anthony smelled of fresh grass, sweat, and blood. His clothing was torn, and there were grass stains along his shoulders and knees. There was a small spot of blood on his shirt. He breathed easily, calmly, staring straight ahead. He didn't appear the least bit upset. This coming from a boy who used to cry if his sister gave him a noogie.

"What happened?" I asked.

"Your son, Ms. Moon, beat up a young man so severely we had to call an ambulance."

I gasped and faced Anthony. Now I could see the tears forming in his eyes. I didn't have much access to my son's thoughts, but I could read auras and body language, not to mention I just knew my son. Knew him better than anyone. And he was scared. Perhaps for what he had done. Perhaps for the harm he had caused. Perhaps for who he was becoming.

The principal continued, "From what I understand—and this has been confirmed by nearly a dozen other students and teachers who witnessed the fight—the school bully, a kid nearly twice the size of your son, and two of his friends were picking on a girl. Grabbing her. Apparently one tried to kiss her. And that's when your son stepped in."

Now my son looked at me for the first time. Tears were in his eyes and there was some dirt in his hairline, but what I saw most was the defiant look in his eyes.

"She was crying, Mommy. She kept asking them to stop. But they wouldn't. They kept picking on her. And no one would help her." He looked forward again, clenching his little fists in his lap. "Everyone's afraid of them, but I'm not."

No one said anything. The principal stared at my son. In complete disbelief, judging by the look on his face. A moment later, the principal continued the story.

Anthony stepped in, pulled the main bully off the girl. And not just *pulled*. Threw, apparently. The other boys jumped my son. The fight was chaotic. Fists swinging, bodies rolling. No one would help. No one would jump in. It was a third grader against three sixth graders. And then something miraculous started happening. One by one, the sixth graders started falling by the wayside, rolling out of the melee, bleeding and groaning and hurt, until finally my son had ended up on top, leveling punch after punch into the older boy's face. It had taken three teachers to pull him off.

The principal's voice trailed off and he looked again at my son with complete awe. Myself, I had never been prouder.

"The leader is in the hospital. Apparently they're stitching his mouth and replacing some teeth."

Outside, I heard some excited voices in the various offices. The principal rubbed his face and kept staring at Anthony. Finally, he sat back in his chair.

"I've never seen or heard anything like this in my twenty years in teaching, Ms. Moon. What your son did...was very brave, very selfless, very admirable. But I have to suspend him."

"For protecting a girl?"

He smiled gently. "For fighting, Ms. Moon. We have a strict policy on that. The other boys will be severely dealt with, trust me. But let's let things cool off for a few days. Your son has caused quite an uproar. And, of course, there could be legal consequences."

A few minutes later, as Anthony and I exited administration offices, I couldn't help but notice everyone staring after us. The principal, secretaries, students and teachers.

Staring at the freaks.

30.

We were at Cold Stone Creamery.

The place was empty. No real surprise there since it was the end of January, still cold even for southern California. Of course, the cold weather didn't stop the sun from searing my skin as I dashed across the parking lot. Now, as Anthony hungrily ate his bowl of ice cream, I sat huddled as far away from the windows as possible.

"I'm sorry, Mommy," said Anthony, in between mouthfuls of ice cream, a masterful concoction of chocolate ice cream, brownies, and Snicker bars, all prepared on a cold stone which, apparently, made the ice cream magical. I wouldn't know, but I think the brownie and Snicker bar had something to do with it.

"Sorry for what?" I asked.

"For fighting."

"Are you sorry for helping the girl?"

"No. She was crying."

"Are you sorry for hurting the boy?"

He thought about that. There was ice cream on his nose. "Well, yes. I didn't mean to hurted him so bad."

"Maybe you can apologize to him someday for hurting him so bad then."

"Okay, Mommy."

He went back to his ice cream, which was nearly gone. How he could eat ice cream so fast, I hadn't a clue. I distinctly recalled a little something called brain freeze. Anthony, apparently, powered through it.

"Tammy tells me that you can wrestle seven boys at once."

"Sometimes ten."

I think my eyes bulged a little, but Anthony was too busy dragging his plastic spoon along the inside edge of the bowl to see my reaction. His little face was the picture of concentration. Ice cream was serious business.

"That's a lot of boys against just one boy, don't you think?"

He shrugged. "I guess. I dunno. Maybe I'm just stronger. Can I have another ice cream?"

"One's enough. I'm making dinner soon."

He stuck out his lower lip the way he does when he wants something. He hardly looked like a kid who just sent the school bully to the hospital.

I said, "Do you like being so strong?"

He gave me a half-assed shrug, since he was

still officially in pouting mode. "It's kinda cool, I guess." Then he began poking his fingers through the Styrofoam bowl and wiggling them at himself, then at me. "Ice cream worms!"

I took the bowl from him. His fingers, I saw, were now covered in chocolate ice cream. He pouted some more.

I said, "Do you wonder why you're so strong?"

He shrugged, though some of his pouting steam was dissipating. "Not really."

I looked at my son. He was still quite little for his age. Too little to be beating up three school punks. Too little to be wrestling a whole group of kids. His dark hair was thick and still a little mussed, no doubt from the fight. He showed no signs of having fought three older boys, although he had put one in the hospital. I suspected a legend was being born about him as we sat here at Cold Stone, whispered throughout school. His life, I suspected, was about to forever change.

No, it changed seven months ago, I thought. *When you changed him.*

When I saved him, goddammit!

I took a deep, shuddering breath. Presently, Anthony was using his fingertip and a few chocolate drips to make shapes on the table. Circles. Happy faces. Sad faces. Such an innocent boy.

What have I done?

"Anthony," I said. "I need to talk to you about something very important."

He looked up, terrified. "But you said you

weren't mad, Mommy."

"I'm not mad, baby. This is about something else."

"About Tammy?"

"What about Tammy?"

"Because she smells so bad?"

And he started giggling, so much so that he passed gas, too. This led to more giggling and a scowl from the Cold Stone manager. And when a wave of gassy foulness hit me, I leaped up from the table, grabbed his hand and we made a mad dash to the minivan, where Anthony continued giggling. Myself included.

Laughing and burning alive.

31.

Anthony knew the drill.

He knew that Mommy had to have the shades drawn in the car. He also knew that Mommy tended to shriek when sunlight hit her directly, so as I faced him in the front seat, as I pulled my knees up and kept my arms out of any direct sunlight, he didn't think much of it. Mommy, after all, was sick.

Or so he thought.

It's time, I thought. *Time to tell him the truth.*

Easier said than done. At least eight different times I opened my mouth to speak, and at least eight different times nothing came out. While I sat there opening and closing my mouth, Anthony played his Gameboy. There was still chocolate on his nose.

I pushed through the nerves and fear and got my mouth working. "Anthony, baby, I need to talk to you about something important—and, no, it's *not* about Tammy's B.O."

He giggled a little, then looked over at me, suddenly serious. "I'm sorry about those boys, Mommy."

"I know you are, honey. Put the Gameboy down. I want to talk to you about something serious, something related to what happened today."

"Related?" he asked, scrunching up his little face.

"It means 'connected.'"

"Like how relatives are connected."

"Yes, that's right. You see, Mommy is..." Except I couldn't finish the sentence. I paused and thought long and hard about the wisdom of continuing it. I paused so long that Anthony looked up at me, squinting with just one eye the way he does sometimes.

He needs to know. He has to know. It's only fair. He can't grow up not knowing. But he's so young. So young...

"Are you okay, Mommy? Is the sun hurting you bad?"

"I'm okay, baby." I took in some air to calm myself, then plunged forward. "Anthony, I'm not like other mommies."

He nodded. "I know. Because you can't go in the sun."

"That's part of it, honey. You see, I'm different in other ways, too. I'm stronger than other mommies."

"Stronger?"

I raised my arm and flexed my bicep, although I don't think much of anything flexed. "Yes, stronger. In fact, I'm stronger than most men, too."

"You mean strong like me," he said.

"Yes."

"Well, duh, Mom. I'm only your kid. Kids have the same stuff their mommies have. But only half of the daddy's."

Now I was confused. "Only half of their daddy's?"

"Duh, Mom. Kids *come* from their mommies, not their daddies."

"I see," I said. "Very logical."

Anthony nodded as if he'd spoken the truth. Then he turned to me, squinting with one eye again. "Is Tammy strong, too?"

"No. She's not like us."

"Why not?"

I shifted in my seat. I wanted to look away. I wanted to avoid his innocent stare. How do you look a little boy in the eye and tell him what I was about to tell him? I didn't know. I didn't know anything. He had to know. He had to. I believed that with all my heart and soul. My dead heart and damned soul.

I said, "Do you remember when you were sick last year?"

My son nodded absently. Mercifully, he looked away and was now playing with the zipper to his jacket.

"Well, last year you were very, very sick, so

141

sick that Mommy had to make you stronger."

"Why?"

"So that you could fight the sickness."

"Oh, cool." He stopped playing with the zipper. He stared at it for a few seconds, then his little face scrunched up the way it does just before he asks a question. "But how did you make me stronger?"

The question I knew he would inevitably ask. Baby steps, I reminded myself. He needed only to be made aware that he was different...and why he was different. Baby steps for now. More later, when he's older.

"I gave you a part of me."

"What part?"

Looking into those round eyes, those red lips, those chubby cheeks...cheeks that were rapidly turning sharper and sharper...I just couldn't do it. I couldn't tell him that he fed from my wrist.

Not yet, I thought. Someday. Perhaps someday soon. Not now. Baby steps.

Instead, I tapped my heart. "I gave you love, baby. All the love I had in the world."

"And it made me stronger?"

"It made you strong like me."

"Wow."

"But this is our secret, okay?"

"Why?"

"Because we're a little different than other people."

"Can I still go in the sun?"

"Yes," I said.

"But how are we different?"

"Well, we are stronger than most people."

"Oh, cool."

"But it's our secret, okay? The way Superman keeps his identity secret."

"And Batman and Spider-Man!"

"Yes, exactly."

"Oh, my gosh! Are we like...superheroes?"

I thought about that. I thought of my son taking care of the school bullies. I thought of myself taking care of Johnny and his gang.

I nodded. "Yeah, a little bit."

"Oh, cool!" He paused and cocked his head a little. "But will I ever be normal again?"

His question hit me by surprise. Maybe I was dreading hearing it. Maybe I had hoped he would never ask it. I looked at him, then looked away. I rubbed my hands together, then ran my fingers through my hair. My son, I knew, would never be normal again. Ever. I was suddenly overwhelmed with what I had done to him.

"Why are you crying, Mommy?"

"I'm sorry, baby."

"Sorry for what?"

So innocent. So sweet. He didn't deserve this. Shit. I started rocking in my seat as my son watched me with wide, concerned eyes. He started patting me on the arm the way he does when he's nervous.

"I'm sorry, Mommy. I'm sorry I made you cry. I didn't mean to."

I covered my face and did my best to hide my

tears, the deep pain that seemed to want to burst from my chest. I held it in. Or tried to.

"I'm so sorry, baby."

"It's okay, Mommy."

And he kept telling me it would be okay, over and over, as I rocked in my seat, weeping into my hands.

32.

On the way home from Cold Stone creamery, I was certain we had picked up a tail.

It was a white cargo van with tinted windows. It had pulled out behind us as we exited the Cold Stone parking lot, then had dropped back four or five car lengths.

Where it held steady.

Until we were about halfway to my house, when it peeled away suddenly. I wouldn't have thought anything of it, except that my inner alarm system had begun buzzing steadily.

A block later, another van appeared behind me. A blue cargo van. Tinted windows. Again five car lengths behind. They were using a tag-team system. I was sure of it. If done right, it's a system that's nearly impossible to detect by the mark.

Except when your mark is a vampire with a highly sensitive inner alarm system. Except when your mark is an ex-federal agent trained to pick up tails.

I made a few random turns, and it kept pace. Anthony turned and looked at me curiously but didn't say anything. Mommy was weird, after all.

I led the van to a quieter street, one with only a single lane, and soon it was directly behind me. I didn't recognize the guy behind the wheel.

Soon, we stopped at a stop sign. Another thing I'd learned to do: reading license plates in my rearview mirror.

Backward.

***

At home, I ran the plate.

The owner was *A-1 Retro Services* out of New Jersey. No address. I did a Google search on A-1 Retro Services and got nothing.

This might seem like a dead end, but it wasn't. It was proof that I had, indeed been followed. In particular, by someone who knew how to stay anonymous. Not hard to do, actually, but it did take some creative accounting.

I stared down at my screen, drummed my fingers, let the information soak in. Ultimately, the question remained: why was I being followed?

I thought about that as I sat back in my office chair and listened to Anthony playing something called Skylanders on his Xbox. Tammy was still at school. I'd arranged with her best friend's mom to

VAMPIRE DAWN

pick her up as well. These days, there were only so many times I could dash out the door and into the sunlight.

Either my condition was getting progressively worse, or I was becoming more monstrous.

Or maybe they were one and the same.

My inner alarm hadn't stopped jangling since we'd gotten home; now, it was just one long, continuous buzz inside my inner ear. Enough to rattle me and keep me on edge.

It's not uncommon for a P.I. to be followed. Granted, it certainly doesn't happen as much as it might in movies or books, but it can happen. The last time I'd been followed was seven months ago, by a handsome, blond-haired vampire hunter with issues. He was last seen heading west on a Carnival Cruise ship to Hawaii, courtesy of yours truly.

So who was out there now? Who was watching me? And why?

The two vans had been driven by experienced surveillance drivers, working in tandem with each other. Now, private eyes piss a lot of people off. Especially cheating husbands and wives.

Except cheating husbands and wives did not use an advanced tag-team surveillance technique.

Down the hallway, in his bedroom, my son laughed loudly. Maybe I shouldn't let him play video games. Maybe a good mother would have punished her son for being suspended from school.

But I just couldn't justify punishing him for helping a girl. Punishing him for doing something *right.*

The inner alarm continued to buzz, so much so that I nearly yelled, "Stop!"

Instead, I got up and paced.

After a few laps, I realized the warning bells were only getting louder.

Jesus, what was happening? What was going to happen?

I didn't know.

Although my psychic abilities had grown, I still could not predict the future. And as I paced my living room, I paused twice to glance out the big living room window that overlooked the front lawn and the cul-de-sac leading up to my house. The cul-de-sac was empty. The street beyond was empty, other than two teenagers sitting on a neighbor's fence, talking and texting.

Random cars were parked here and there.

No sign of any cargo vans.

The buzzing between my ears sounded like a swarm of gnats circling my head. I nearly swatted at them, like King Kong swatting at airplanes on top of the Empire State Building.

I forced myself to sit on my couch, forced myself to take deep breaths, to calm down. I focused on my breathing.

There. Easy now. Calm down.

And from this state of semi-tranquility, I closed my eyes and was able to cast my thoughts out like a net. An ever-widening net that trawled through my house, through the different rooms, and out into the back yard—

Where I saw two men creeping through my back yard.

They were both armed with crossbows.

I gasped and snapped back into my body, just as glass broke from down the hallway.

Anthony's room.

33.

I stumbled off the couch, disoriented and dizzy, braced myself on a wall, then hurtled through my small house.

"Anthony!" I screamed.

I was in my son's room in a blink, and what I saw took a second or two to absorb. The bedroom window was broken. The sound of running feet. My son standing there in the center of his room, breathing hard, fists clenched.

"It's okay, Mommy. They're gone now."

I looked my son over wildly, then hurried over to the broken window. Our house abuts the Pep Boys parking lot, separated by our backyard fence. From inside the house, I could just see a white van peeling away from the fence, zigzagging briefly.

Sweet Jesus.

I considered pursuing, but there was no way in

hell was I leaving my son. I noted the broken glass wasn't inside the bedroom, as I had expected. The glass was outside, littering the dry grass, sparkling there under the last of the setting sun. A sun that was even now burning me alive.

I fought through it, grimacing, trying to piece together what had happened. The glass was broken out, which meant...

And then I saw it, a few feet away. Anthony's Xbox controller was lying in the grass, too, broken into two or three pieces.

He had thrown it. Through the window. I looked back at my son. But he wasn't looking at me. He simply stood in the center of the room, fists clenched, looking out through the broken window.

"What happened, Anthony?"

"There were two of them," he said calmly. He did not sound like my little boy. He sounded years older. "I saw them climb over the wall. One of them looked in the window."

"And you threw your controller at him." My voice, still shocked, was now full of something close to awe. "Through the window?"

He nodded. "It hit him in the face. He screamed and fell down. When he got up, he was bleeding bad. I think some glass was in his face. Maybe his nose was broken."

Holy shit.

"Then both of them ran off again. They jumped the wall, and that's when you came in."

My God.

"You need to get out of the sun, Mommy."

My son took my hand and led me away, out of his room and into the hallway. I could smell my own burning flesh. If I looked hard enough, I might even see steam rising off my skin.

I said, gasping, "Are you okay, honey?"

"Of course, Mommy."

I pulled my son in close and held him tight. Two men with crossbows. Vampire hunters. Here at my house. Following me.

"Who were those men, Mommy?"

"Bad men."

"Were they robbers?"

I nodded but didn't say anything. I pulled him in closer, and we stood like that in the hallway, holding each other tight, while the cool wind came in through the broken window, rattled the blinds, and eventually found us huddling together in the hallway.

34.

Have you pissed anyone off lately, Moon Dance?

It was nearly midnight, and, after working with a 24-hour glass service, I had contacted Fang and gotten him up to speed.

No more than usual, I wrote.

And you're sure one of them wasn't our vampire hunter from last year?

I shook my head, although I was alone in the room. *I'm fairly certain. Randolph the vampire hunter worked alone, and this was a two-man crew. Besides, Randolph and I are on good terms.*

Meaning what?

Meaning, I'm not very high on his kill list.

Randolph the vampire hunter doesn't sound very catchy.

Maybe not, but he's effective.

I still say you shoulda dropped his ass in the

ocean. Why leave it to chance that he might return?

A judgment call.

A judgment call you might regret, he wrote, paused, then added: *Sorry, Moon Dance. I'm just very, very protective of you, and two creeps showing up at your house with fucking crossbows scares the shit out of me. I mean, what if they had gotten a shot off at you, or your son?*

It was nearly too horrible to contemplate, so I didn't. Fang sensed this and changed the subject a little.

Have you talked to Anthony about, well, everything?

Mostly. I told him that we were different. I told him that we were stronger than most people. He said something about being superheroes, and I went with that for now.

Except that might do more damage than good, Moon Dance.

For now, it's enough that he knows he's different and needs to keep it secret.

Baby steps, wrote Fang, obviously reading my mind.

Yes, baby steps. Also...

But I couldn't finish the thought. I stopped writing, but Fang, privy to my thoughts, had picked up on it. He finished it for me, writing: *Also, you're tired of hiding who you are.*

Yes.

Will you tell your daughter?

I think so. Yes.

How do you think they will take it?

I don't know, Fang. I only hope they don't hate me.

Well, I, for one, would think you were the coolest mom ever.

Yeah, well, you're also a freak.

I could almost hear Fang chuckling lightly on his end. On my end, I could hear Anthony snoring lightly and faint music issuing from Tammy's room. The house creaked from somewhere and I nearly bolted to my feet.

Just the house settling. Calm down, Sam.

Easier said than done.

Earlier, Kingsley had offered to come over, but the big guy had an important court hearing in the morning, and I assured him I would be fine. Fang had offered, too, but I politely declined. Truth was, I doubted they would be back. Whoever they were, the element of surprise was gone. If they were going to attack, they were going to do it somewhere else.

And just who were they?

That was the question of the hour.

A minute or two passed before the pencil icon appeared again in the chatbox window, indicating Fang was typing a message, followed by: *I've been doing some research into blood dealers, Moon Dance.*

Oh?

He shielded his thoughts while he typed out his response. He didn't want me to know his sources, which was fine by me. We all had our secrets.

Apparently, there's a sort of hierarchy to blood.

What do you mean?

Degrees of desirability. For instance, animal blood is the lowest. Deceased human blood is next.

I recalled Detective Hanner's comment about gathering blood from morgues and hospitals. I shuddered.

I wrote, *And fresh human blood is the most desirable.*

Not quite, Moon Dance.

What do you mean?

There's another source of blood that's even more desirable than human blood. Vampire blood. Apparently, Moon Dance, your blood fetches a pretty penny on the open market.

Jesus.

I suspect Robert Mason is far more dangerous than you realize.

35.

We were cuddling in front of an 80-inch Sharp flat screen TV, which was a little like cuddling in front of a portal into the fourth dimension.

The room was also equipped with surround sound speakers which made the sound seem to magically appear as if from nowhere. To this day, I haven't a clue where those speakers are embedded. Most important, the room came equipped, at least part time, with a beast of a man who, despite his size, was a helluva cuddler.

We were cuddling and watching Matt Damon's latest spy thriller when Kingsley turned to me and asked, "Would you like a drink?"

If he was offering wine or water, he would have said wine or water. *Drink* was Kingsley-speak for a very different kind of red stuff: blood.

I sat up, reached for the remote, and paused the movie.

"It's really a simple yes-or-no question, Sam," he said good-naturedly. Kingsley was wearing a t-shirt and workout pants, and both were filled to capacity. It took a lot of man to fill out an oversized pair of workout pants, but somehow Kingsley managed to do it. He also smelled of Old Spice. Simple. Manly. Yummy.

I turned to him. "May I first ask where you got your *drink*?"

He rolled his eyes. "Jesus, Sam. I thought we discussed that."

"No. You gave me a song and dance about vampires using various willing and unwilling donors. So, tell me, was this a willing donor? I think I have a right to know who I'm consuming, don't you think?"

He turned and looked at me, his thick hair following over one shoulder. "Boy, I didn't see this coming."

Truth was, I didn't either. At least, I hoped it wouldn't. I knew there was a killer out there supplying blood, and I knew my current boyfriend purchased blood from...someone.

"If not tonight," I said. "Then another night. I need to know."

On the wall before us, Matt Damon used some impressive fight moves—and a lot of editing—to kick the unholy crap out of a spy that looked remarkably like a popular Hollywood star. In the kitchen nearby, I heard Franklin the butler humming to himself. Kingsley's resident freak had a surprisingly sweet voice.

Kingsley said, "I buy the blood from a trusted supplier."

I couldn't read the mind of another immortal, but I didn't need to be a mind-reader to know who he was talking about. I said, "Detective Hanner."

His lower jaw dropped a little. For a man who was legendary for keeping his cool, this statement caught him by surprise. And it was all the admission I needed.

"How long has she been supplying you?" I asked.

He cracked his neck a little. Clearly uncomfortable. So much for openness in a relationship. "A number of years, Sam. I normally keep only a small amount on hand."

"And here's the million-dollar question, babe," I said. "Where does Hanner get her blood?"

"Donors."

"Willing donors?"

"Jesus, Sam. You're closer friends with her than I am these days. You tell me."

I shook my head. "You've known her a lot longer. Hell, you're even a *customer*."

Kingsley stood in one motion, so quickly that it boggled the mind. One smooth motion. Like a spring being sprung. "Look, Sam. I'm not keeping anything from you. It's just that your kind and my kind don't generally discuss this topic."

"The topic of blood?"

"Right."

"It's taboo," I said.

"Sam, we all have skeletons in our closets. Especially us." By "us," I knew he was talking about creatures of the night. "I have them, you have them. We all have them. We couldn't exist without collecting them."

"So, what's your point?"

"We don't dig too deeply into each other's lives, Sam. Dig deep enough into mine and you might not like what you find. And if I dig deep enough into yours, even in the short time you've been a vampire, I might not like what I find, either."

"So you just stick your head in the sand?"

"Sometimes, it's best not to know, Sam."

I shook my head. "Real people are getting killed out there. Real people with lives and families and hopes and dreams. Slaughtered for blood. It's not right."

"Of course it's not right." He put his hand on my knee. "Let it go, Sam, okay? She's not a killer. She's one of us."

I did not let it go. Could not let it go. The rest of the Matt Damon movie was lost on me, and as I absently watched the fight scenes, the chase scenes, and the bevy of cute buns, all I could think about was one person.

Detective Hanner.

36.

It was just after 9 p.m., and I was going through the missing person list again.

A sad list, to be sure.

The files were, of course, peppered with photos of the missing. Driver's license pictures, family pictures, Christmas pictures. Pictures of couples holding hands. Pictures with co-workers. Only a small fraction of the missing were children. Three, in fact. Most of the missing were adults, and most were in their twenties.

In all, there were fifty-three missing-person cases in Orange County over a five-year span. Higher than even Los Angeles County, which, by my calculations, only had forty-one in the same period. And Los Angeles was nearly three times the size of Orange County.

That, in and of itself, was startling evidence.

There was an epidemic of missing people in

Orange County, and so far, nothing had been made of it.

I studied the many pictures, trying to get a feel for them. Sometimes, I got blurry flashes, but the pictures and the files were too cold, too copied, too informal. Too old.

Over the past seven months, I'd enjoyed many goblets of fresh hemoglobin at Kingsley's and Hanner's. Looking at these files now, seeing these pictures now, spread before me in my living room, I was beginning to suspect with mounting horror that the blood I had consumed, the blood that had nourished my body, the blood that I had *relished*, belonged to these people.

Sweet Jesus.

Of course, I didn't know that for sure. Truth was, I didn't know what the hell was going on. Hanner had told me repeatedly the blood was from willing donors. But some of it was and maybe some of it wasn't. Maybe that was enough for her to lie to my face.

I was sitting cross-legged in the center of my living room, immersed in the missing. Having these files was highly illegal, which is why I had discreetly copied them while Sherbet had been on a curiously long coffee break. Just long enough, interestingly, for me to copy all the files.

So here I was now, late in the evening, scouring the files like my life depended on it. And maybe it did. Two men with crossbows suggested it did. Fang's recent revelation of the high desirability of vampire blood suggested it did.

Which was why my kids were presently staying with my sister, Mary Lou—which is where they would stay until I felt it was safe to bring them home again.

That Robert Mason was connected to all of this, I had no doubt. Sherbet agreed. For a case like this, a search warrant would do wonders. A suspect's home was thoroughly searched, and such searches usually turned up something, especially if the suspect was guilty.

Unless, of course, the suspect was an ex-soap opera star with a small amount of fame. A judge was going to be extremely careful handing out a search warrant.

Unless I could find something connecting Robert Mason to another victim.

Or, in this case, to a missing person.

I looked down at the dozens of files spread before me. Somewhere in this mosaic of the missing, this patchwork of faces and files, was the evidence I needed.

I was sure of it.

So, I closed my eyes and took a deep breath, exhaled and expanded my consciousness out, touching down on each file. In my mind's eye, I saw a ball of light. I then slowly, carefully, opened my eyes and the ball of light remained, floating above the files.

This was weird. A damn new experience for me. Anything psychic before was generally done with my eyes closed.

I had created that light somehow. Could others see it? I didn't know, but I doubted it.

Either way, I watched as this ball of light moved over the floor methodically, like a slow-moving unmanned spy drone.

I kept breathing calmly, easily.

The ball of light neared the outer edge of the files. Maybe this was a lame idea. This psychic stuff was still so new to me. Or maybe I was barking up the wrong tree. Maybe the missing in California had nothing to do with Robert Mason.

Maybe. Calm. Relax.

The fiery ball in my mind's eye had begun to break up as my own thoughts grew more and more scattered. But I focused them again, and watched. And waited.

The light paused over a file. As it did so, a very strong knowing came over me. That's the one. As if on cue, the ball of light began descending, until it finally rested on the file.

And then the light disappeared.

I gasped and reached for the file.

37.

At first blush, there wasn't much here.

A twenty-two-year-old male. Missing since last year. No evidence that he'd ever worked for the Fullerton Playhouse, or that he was involved in acting in any way. In fact, he was a computer salesman at Best Buy in Fullerton. His name was Gabriel Friday, and he was last seen going to work.

Except he never made it.

That was sixteen months ago.

Again, not much there. Of course, I didn't need much. I just needed a connection to Robert Mason. As I flipped through the file, there was no surprise that Sherbet and I didn't see one here. There was nothing obvious here. Nothing that would indicate a connection of any kind.

Maybe I was wrong. After all, who trusts random balls of light?

I did.

I shoved the file into a folder, checked the time on my cell, then headed out to Best Buy. In the least, I could finally see what the hell a Nook was.

***

The Best Buy night manager in Fullerton was a black woman named Shelley, who was shorter than me and looked far tougher. She led me to a small office behind the help desk and showed me to a seat in front of a metal desk.

"So you're a private investigator?" she asked, easing around the desk.

"That's what it says on my tax returns."

She smiled easily. I suspected her easy smile could turn serious fast. "I've always wanted to be a private investigator. In a way, part of my job involves in-house investigations. Missing money. Missing shipments. Missing merchandise. Last month, I caught two employees loading up a minivan with Dyson vacuums."

"They're nice vacuums," I said. "Almost worth going to jail over."

She laughed. "And that's exactly where they are now."

"You're kind of a badass."

She leveled her considerable stare at me. "I'm a lot of badass, honey," she said. "Maybe we should team up someday and fight crime together."

I grinned. I liked her. A lot. "Our first order of business could be to take down an international vacuum syndicate."

"With stakeouts?"

"Of course."

"You've got yourself a deal." She smiled. "Now, how can I help you, Ms. Moon?"

"I'm here about Gabriel Friday."

"Gabriel. Was he found?"

I shook my head. "Not yet. I'm sorry."

She was about to say something, then closed her mouth again. She nodded once, and I saw that she was, in fact, trying to control herself.

"Were you close to him?" I asked.

"I try to be close to all my workers, Ms. Moon."

"Please, call me Samantha."

She nodded. "Very well, Samantha. Yes, as close as a manager and computer geek could be. We talked as much as time would allow, which might only be a few minutes a week, but I always make the effort."

"You said 'geek'? A term of endearment?"

"A job title. He was part of the Geek Squad, our mobile support techs."

"I see," I said, and now my mind was racing.

She dried her eyes and looked at me directly. "Why do you ask about him, Samantha?"

I shifted in my seat. "I have reason to believe that his disappearance might be related to another case."

I liked Shelley. She deserved the truth, no matter how hard it was for me to tell her. When I was finished, she ran both hands through her thick hair, then just kept them there, holding her head. She seemed instantly lost.

"I'm sorry," I said.

"Oh, sweet Jesus. He was such a good kid, such a good kid. He didn't deserve this. I got to know his mother through all of this. They weren't close, and had a falling out, but she loved him so much. Missed him so much. We were all looking for answers. This can't be the answer."

As she buried her face in her hands, I moved over to her side and put my arm around her shoulder as she wept quietly for a few moments. I gently patted her shoulder and thought to myself that everyone should be so lucky to have a boss who cared so much.

When she had gotten control of herself, blowing her nose on a tissue and sitting a little straighter, I moved back around the desk and asked if she still had records of Gabriel's clients.

She nodded. "I kept everything after his disappearance. Wasn't sure what would be important or not."

She had good instincts. I said, "Did the police go through the records?"

She nodded. "Cursory at best. They looked at them, but as far as I know, that's all they did."

"And what's in the files?"

"Just routine stuff. Records of various house calls. Sometimes to businesses, too."

"Businesses?"

"Yes."

"May I see his file?"

"Of course, honey."

She spun her chair around and rolled over to a big filing cabinet in the far corner of the office. There, she dug through the first drawer until she came out with a thickish folder.

"Everything's in here," she said, rolling back, setting it in front of me. "The service orders and final receipts. Not to mention his evaluations and anything else we had on him."

"Thank you," I said.

"If you need any help, Samantha Moon, you let me know. I would personally like to bring this piece of shit down, whoever he is."

"I'll keep you in mind."

She held my gaze a moment longer, and I think the two of us might have bonded. When she was gone, I cracked the file open. It took me precisely two minutes to find a service order for the Fullerton Playhouse.

Called in by Robert Mason himself.

38.

Sherbet answered on the first ring.

"First-ring relationships are serious business," I said.

"Don't get used to it, kid. I just kinda, you know, *sensed* you were going to call me. Or something like that."

I laughed. "Why, Detective, you sound kind of freaky."

He growled under his breath, which nearly made my phone vibrate against my ear. This was all new to Sherbet. After all, homicide detectives don't sense things. They operate on facts and evidence. At best, they might get an informed hunch.

"So what's the news, Sam? Out with it."

I told him about the file, about my trip to Best Buy, and about the missing tech guy. Although I still wasn't sure what the hell a Nook was, I had discovered that Robert Mason had hired the missing tech.

"Good work, and what's this Nook thing you're talking about?"

"I haven't said anything about a Nook. You're reading my thoughts again, Detective."

More growling. "What's this tech's name again?"

"Gabriel Friday."

"Hang on. I've got his file somewhere...okay, here it is."

I had no doubt that Sherbet's home office looked similar to mine, stacked with files and reports. I soon heard him flipping through pages. He paused in his flipping—reading, no doubt—then said, "Okay, so it says the kid disappeared on his way to work."

"Yes."

"And phone records indicate he received an unknown call just prior to coming in to work."

"Says the same thing in my file," I said.

"Probably because you illegally copied the file," said Sherbet. "So, what are you thinking, Sam?"

"I'm thinking Robert Mason gave Gabriel a call."

"Maybe asked him to swing by the theater early one morning, perhaps to fix a bug in the computer."

"Something like that," I said. "Sort of a follow-up call."

"Gabriel's car—a VW bug—was found burned out in Corona," said Sherbet.

"Near where Brian Meeks's body was found."

Sherbet paused, no doubt reading the same information I was reading. "Within a few miles, actually."

"Yup."

"So Gabriel Friday shows up to give Robert Mason a helping hand...maybe do some pro bono work to help out the local theater...and Mason offs him," said Sherbet.

"And drains him of blood."

"Jesus," said the detective. "I'll call you back in a few minutes."

He called me back, in fact, in fifteen minutes.

"I got it," he said.

"Got what?"

"The search warrant. We're going in tonight."

"Going in where?"

"His house."

"What about the theater?"

"The warrant only covers the house and any outbuildings on the property. The theater isn't on the property."

"But he owns it."

"Let's take it one property at a time, Sam."

"Fine. I want to go with you tonight."

"You can't, Sam. You know that. Official police business and all that."

"Then do me one favor," I said.

"This have anything to do with Hanner? Why did I just say that?"

"Because I gave you a peek into my thoughts."

I gave him another peek. In particular, I gave

him access to my suspicions about Hanner.

"I don't understand, Sam," said Sherbet. "What's this got to do with Hanner?"

I next showed him an image—my own memory, really—of Hanner and myself on the deck of her house. Drinking blood. Together.

Sherbet didn't say anything for a long time. So long that I wondered if the old geezer had fallen asleep. But I knew he was working this through.

Finally, in a voice so deep that it nearly rattled my teeth, he said, "How did I not know, Sam? I feel like an idiot."

"It's a gift of hers, Detective. She can plant thoughts and, I think, alter thoughts. In the least, divert thoughts."

"Can you do this, too?"

"I...I don't know."

"So, as far as I know, this whole damn city could be full of vampires, and I wouldn't know. No one would know. Because anytime one of us gets a whiff of a vampire, they put a subliminal thought in our head to order a Starbucks instead."

"Sounds like a valid conspiracy."

"This isn't funny, Sam. I'm seriously freaked out here. I mean, a bloody fucking vampire has been working under my nose for, what, five or six years, and I hadn't a clue."

"Don't be too hard on yourself, Detective. Remember, you sniffed me out pretty quick."

"Not really. I just thought you were damn weird."

"Something every girl wants to hear."

"You know what I mean, Sam. You had my radar pinging. Detective Hanner...nothing. Not even a suspicion. And she even works the goddamn night shift."

"She's an old vampire, Detective. Old enough, I think, to know a few tricks."

"Worse," said Sherbet, "is that I like her. Legitimately like her."

"So do I."

"Fine," he said. "I'll conduct this tonight without her. I'll round up a few of our boys and hit this house hard. I'll call you when it's over."

And he disconnected the line.

39.

I had just set aside my cell phone when there came a loud knock at my front door. Loud and obnoxious.

And since my inner alarm was not ringing, I relaxed a little as I moved through the hallway. Still, if there was a vampire hunter on the other side of that door, he was in for one hellacious fight.

It wasn't.

As I glanced through the peep hole, I saw a wildly warped and misshapen, yet familiarly handsome, face.

Fang.

His face, if possible, appeared even more misshapen due to what he was holding in his right hand: a bottle of hooch. I opened the door and he veritably spilled into my living room.

"Hope I'm not disturbing you or anything, Moon Dance," he said, catching himself on the center post that divided the foyer from the living room. His speech was nearly incoherent.

"You're drunk, Fang."

"Oh, am I? I thought I was just shit-faced."

I shut the door and double locked it behind me. As I did so, Fang began whistling for a dog. "Here, wolfie. Here, boy."

"Kingsley's not here," I said, irritated.

"Oh, that's a shame...I had brought him some bones from work. Ribs, I think." He briefly held up a greasy bag, which he shoved back into his coat pocket.

"You're being a jerk, Fang."

He stood before me, swaying slightly. "You'll have to forgive me, Moon Dance. I've kind of been dealing with a broken heart."

Fang wasn't looking too well. His hair looked dirty. His clothing was wrinkled. His hygiene was questionable. He also looked like he'd lost about ten pounds since I'd last seen him.

He held up his bottle of booze. Vodka. A big bottle, too, and it was nearly empty. "Would you like a drink, Moon Dance?"

"What are you doing here, Fang?"

"Oh, that's right. Vampires can't drink the hard stuff. Only the red stuff." He laughed a little too hard at his own joke, then pushed away from the center post and stumbled into the adjoining living room. Like I said, I live in a small house. With two or three steps, a person could go from the foyer, to the dining room, to the living room.

"You mind if I sit, Moon Dance? I'm not feeling too well."

As he stumbled across the floor, I ran to his side and helped him down onto my beautiful new couch. Once there, I positioned him so that his boots hung off the edge. I also relieved him of the vodka bottle.

As I positioned a pillow under him, he watched me with big, wet eyes. They were beautiful eyes. Knowing eyes. Drunk eyes. "Ah, Moon Dance. It almost feels as if you care about me."

"Of course I care about you, Fang."

I went into the kitchen, poured the booze down the drain, and deposited the bottle in my recycle bag. When I came back, Fang was trying to remove his boots. I knew that the drunk bastard would have to sleep it off here. Sighing, I helped him with his boots. Once again, he watched me. This time with a big, stupid, drunk grin.

"I like when you help me, Moon Dance. It feels good."

"Yeah, well, you smell like greasy ribs and vodka and its turning my stomach."

"Words every man wants to hear." He patted the area next to him on the couch. "Lay next to me, Moon Dance."

"No."

"Why not?"

"Because it's not right."

"Hey, if you're not going to turn me into a blood-sucking fiend, then at least throw me a few crumbs here, Sam. Something, anything."

"If you're going to talk like this, Fang, then I'm calling you a cab."

"Talk like what, Moon Dance? Affectionately? Lustfully? I loved you long before your shaggy wolf friend came sniffing around. I poured my heart out to you. Gave you all my attention. All my love, even if it was from afar. How many times did I drop everything to help you? How many times did I forego my own needs to help you, to talk to you, to be there for you?"

"You stalked me, Fang."

"It was the only way, Moon Dance. The only way. You would not have come out into the light. Literally."

"I would have. Someday."

"But not soon enough, obviously. I waited too long, and look what happened. *Aroooooo*."

"You're drunk, Fang."

"But that makes my pain no less real, Samantha Moon. I loved you like no other, and you tossed me aside for your doggie toy. The least you could do was turn me, to make me like you, to help ease the pain."

"You're trying to manipulate me, to make me feel guilty, Fang, and that's a shitty thing to do."

"It's nothing but the truth, Moon Dance."

"Get some sleep, Fang."

Indeed, his eyes were dropping fast. He turned on his side and wrapped an arm around himself and I saw something disturbing at his wrists. Fresh wounds. Bite marks. Had he been biting himself again? I didn't know.

I stared down at Fang, a man I legitimately cared for and loved on some level. A man for whom I had no answers. That he was miserable, there was no doubt. That he loved me in his own way, I had no doubt either.

What I should do about it all, I still didn't know.

Soon after he was snoring loudly into one of the couch cushions, I decided to follow up on a hunch.

I grabbed my stuff and headed out the door.

40.

I was looking down from a roof top, watching the Fullerton Playhouse below.

It was windy up here, and my light jacket flapped wildly. Too wildly. I think I was losing weight. A steady diet of blood will do that to you.

I was kneeling on the roof's corner, four stories up. Directly below me was a bank. Why a bank needed four floors, I hadn't a clue. Sure as hell wasn't to store my money. So far there was no movement below, although I had spotted something very interesting in the alley behind the theater.

A blue cargo van.

I waited and watched. Other than the van, the theater looked empty. There was no movement. No lights. It was well past time for any rehearsals and any cleaning crews.

I decided not to make a move, unless something prompted me to. I was here for one reason only: to keep an eye on the theater, should the shit hit the fan. Or should someone get tipped off about the police raid.

So far, all was quiet.

My cell phone chimed. A text message. I glanced at the screen. A text message from Danny.

Thanks, Sam! They didn't come back to collect from me. Whatever you did, I owe you one.

"You owe me two, loser," I whispered, and erased his message.

I was dressed in jeans and the aforementioned light jacket. There had been an old fire escape that I had managed to grab onto. Now, I waited and watched. Just another mom with two kids, waiting on the roof of a bank building for a serial killer to emerge from his creepy theater.

Perhaps an hour later my cell vibrated.

I picked up on the first vibration which, I think, was the equivalent to a single ring. It was, of course, Detective Sherbet.

"Mason wasn't there," he said.

"Go figure," I said. "Anything turn up?"

"Nothing yet, but my guys are working on it. If there's a blood stain anywhere, they'll find it."

"Except if he's as good at killing as I suspect, then there's not going to be any evidence at his home."

"What are you saying, Sam?"

"He kills at the theater, Detective. You know that, I know that. He kills and drains and bottles his victims' blood all at the theater."

"A blood factory."

"Or a slaughtering house. A human slaughtering house."

"Jesus, Sam." Sherbet paused. "Then why not destroy the bodies there?"

"Maybe he does. Or maybe he *usually* does. Maybe he ran out of room. Or maybe he's decided to make it a bit of a game."

"Jesus, Sam. I'm too old for this shit."

"We have to stop him, Detective."

Sherbet paused again, said, "We've got another missing person reported tonight. A female. Twenty-three. Last seen leaving class at Fullerton College two nights ago."

"She's there," I said, with a surety that wasn't psychic. It was my gut. My investigator's instincts. "The son-of-a-bitch has her. And my bet is she's somewhere behind that door."

"We can't just go in there, Sam."

"Perhaps you can't, but I can."

"Sam, wait."

"What?"

He exhaled loudly and if I truly wanted to I could have followed his entire train of thought. Instead, I gave him his privacy, let him work this out on his own. Finally, after exhaling again, he said, "I'm coming with you."

"Welcome aboard, Detective."

41.

We met behind the theater.

Sherbet was wearing jeans and a leather jacket that barely covered his roundish mid-section. He was also sporting dark-leather shoes that looked like a cross between running shoes and hiking shoes. I knew he was packing heat, and the truth was, I felt better having him here. Sherbet exuded an aura of control and security. More so than any man I'd ever met, even Kingsley.

I might be a creature of the night who has faced my share of monsters, but sneaking into the dragon's lair alone just sounded like one hell of a shitty way to spend an evening.

The alley parking lot was empty, with only a single spotlight shining down on the back door. A sticker claimed that there was an alarm system in use, but we were about to see. I doubted there was. If this place was what I thought it was, then I doubted Mr. Robert Mason ever wanted the police anywhere near the premises. If anything, he would handle the intruders himself.

Not to mention, Mason had help. Two goons had shown up at my house and neither had been Mason, I was sure of it. Three against two. I liked our chances.

I doubted Hanner was directly involved in the production of the blood. She seemed more refined than that. She seemed...better than that. What her connection was, exactly, I didn't know.

But I was going to find out.

I was the first to try the door. Locked, of course. I turned the lever a little harder, and it broke free in my hand. "It's not really breaking in," I said, holding up the broken handle. "If the door is broken, right?"

Sherbet shook his head and eased his bulk around me. As he did so, I had a momentary whiff of Old Spice and sweat, which, for me, was one hell of a heady mixture. "We're not breaking in," he growled, as he broke in. "This is an emergency search. There's a young woman missing, and he's our only suspect. I'm sticking to that story until the day I die."

"Sounds good to me."

He removed his Smith & Wesson from his shoulder holster. "C'mon."

The hallway was pitch black to anyone but me. To me, it was alive and alight. Sherbet reached into a pocket and removed a small flashlight that had a lot of *umph* to it, revealing a narrow hallway with a door to either side.

"Lights?" I asked.

Sherbet shook his head and continued sweeping the powerful beam over walls and floors and ceilings. "I don't want anyone running; at least, not yet. We'll catch the bastards by surprise."

"Sounds like my last date."

Sherbet grinned. "Sure it does. So what are we looking for?"

"A storage room. Or a props rooms. We're close to it, I think."

"Then what?"

"We look for a mirror."

"A mirror?"

"Yes."

"And you know this how?"

"I'm a freaky chick."

He rolled his eyes. "Fine. Then what?"

"There should be an opening behind it."

"Thank God you didn't say *through it*. Dealing with vampires is bad enough. I don't think I can handle Harry Potter, too." Sherbet took another step, then paused. "Hey, do that crazy thing you do with your mind."

"My mind?"

"You know, one of those mental scouting jobs you do, or whatever you call it."

"'Mental scouting job' sounds good to me," I said. "Give me a moment."

"I'll give you two."

I closed my eyes, exhaled, and cast my thoughts out like a net. The net scattered throughout the theater, through rooms and offices, across the stage and theater seating, and even up into the lighting booth.

"We're alone up here," I said, reporting back, opening my eyes. "Except for the ghosts."

"What ghosts?"

"The ghosts that have been following us since we stepped foot in here."

"I didn't need to know that."

Lots of old places have spirits hanging around them, and this theater, which was decades old, if not a century, was no exception. Still, there seemed to be a lot of spirit energy here, more than to be expected, energy which flitted past quickly, energy which appeared and disappeared next to us, energy which watched us from the shadows. Some of the energy fully manifested into lightly glowing human forms. These watched us from doorways and rafters, from behind curtains and in windows. I decided not to tell Sherbet about the entity standing next to him. For a tough guy, he sure got the willies over ghosts.

"You said alone up here," said Sherbet. "You think this creep works below ground?"

"Would be my guess."

"And your radar whatchamacallit doesn't pick up Mason?"

"Not yet."

"Which means?"

"We're still probably too far from him."

"Or that the place is empty."

"We'll see," I said.

"Fine. C'mon."

We soon found ourselves somewhere backstage, where backdrops hung from flies and where trap doors were cleverly placed in the floor. Clothing racks filled with costumes lined both sides of the wall, and a catwalk ran along the upper levels. There were many, many ghosts moving back and forth along these metal walkways.

Lots of death here.

And, judging by the many gashes in their necks, lots of victims here, too. I kept this last assessment to myself. I suspected Sherbet was about to see for himself just what was going on here.

We found a hallway leading off to one side of the stage, which we followed to the props room. The door was ajar.

"This is it," I said.

Sherbet nodded and slipped inside first, holding the gun out in front of him even though we were alone in the theater. I think it made him feel manly. Not to mention, he was still a cop, and cops did these kinds of things.

I paused at the doorway, taking in the room despite the darkness. The room was, of course, exactly as I had seen it in my mind days earlier. Props of all shapes and sizes, everything from dinner tables and jukeboxes to plastic trees and park benches. Like a small town all crammed into one room.

I pointed to the far wall. "There."

Sherbet followed my finger, aiming his light, and illuminated a massive mirror that was apparently attached to the wall.

"The mirror. Just like you said."

"Yep."

"And you've never been here before?"

"Nope. At least, not physically."

"This is crazy."

"Welcome to my life."

He shook his head and I heard his thoughts, despite my best attempts to stay out of them. Rather clearly, Sherbet thought: *I'm going insane.*

The scent of blood suddenly wafted over me, coming from the far wall—from behind the mirror, no doubt. My traitorous stomach growled instantly. So loudly that Sherbet turned and looked at me. I shrugged innocently.

As we moved around a four-poster bed covered in cobwebs, Sherbet said, "I swear to God that if a guy in a hockey mask and a chainsaw starts singing about the music, I'm going to start shooting."

"You're mixing, I think, like three movies together."

"Well, they've been warned."

We found ourselves at the big mirror. The smell of blood was most definitely coming from somewhere behind the mirror. I said as much to Sherbet, even as my stomach growled again.

Sherbet looked at me, looked at the mirror, then

looked at my stomach. He put two and two together and grimaced unconsciously. Finally, he said, "Help me with the mirror."

He holstered his gun and we each took one side of the mirror and lifted it off the hook. Once done, we set it to one side, and returned to the spot where the mirror had hung.

There was, of course, a door there.

A hidden door.

42.

The scent of blood was nearly overwhelming.

So much blood.

Sherbet and I had the same thought simultaneously: to scan the room beyond. So I did so, and saw that it was empty of anything living. I reported my findings to Sherbet.

He nodded and pointed at the doorknob. "Any chance this lock is broken as well?"

I reached for the doorknob and a moment later dropped the twisted metal to the floor. "I would say a good chance."

He shook his head. "I'm just glad you're on our side. C'mon."

He eased the door open, which promptly groaned loudly on rusted hinges. He flashed his light on the ancient, rusted hinges. He said, "My guess is there's another way down here. Probably accessible from the alley."

"Would make it easier bringing bodies in and out."

Sherbet nodded grimly. He next swept his light around the small room. "Another storage room."

I was suddenly having difficulty focusing on the detective's words. After all, the scent of blood was much stronger in here. Much, much stronger. And intoxicating.

Doing my best to ignore it, I stepped in behind Sherbet and saw that the room was filled to overflowing with even more theater junk. Moldy props. Moldy clothing. Hats that were badly destroyed by rats or moths. Boxes and crates and old furniture. And the moment I stepped inside, my inner alarm began buzzing.

"What's that sound?" asked Sherbet, pausing, listening.

"What sound?"

"You can't hear it? It's a steady buzzing. Like electricity crackling."

Stunned that the detective could pick up on my own inner alarm, and stunned at the depth of our connection, I told him what he was hearing.

"Thank God. Thought I was going crazy all over again. C'mon, let's check this out, and be careful. It's buzzing for a reason."

The air was alive with frenetic energy, which lit the way for me. Not so much for Sherbet. His flashlight would have to do. Tiny claws scrabbled in the far corner of the small room. A mouse or a rat.

By all appearances this was just a forgotten

storage room. A storage room hidden purposely by a massive mirror. If I had to guess, I would say the crap in here hadn't seen the light of day—or the light of the stage—for over fifty years.

Most important: it appeared to have no exit.

We moved deeper into the room. Sherbet's breathing filled the small space. Mine, not so much. The wooden floorboards groaned under the big detective's weight. Me, not so much. The smell of blood was heady and distracting and reminding me all over again just what a monster I had become. Sherbet gave no indication of being able to smell the blood.

The metallic scent wafted through the far wall of the room, that much was clear. I moved toward the wall, toward the smell. Once there, I reached out a hand and placed it on the cool wood paneling. With Sherbet easing up behind me, I closed my eyes and cast my thoughts outward again. This time my trawling consciousness returned images of a short corridor and wooden stairs that descended down. At the base of the stairs, I saw another door. I tried to push through that...but the images beyond were vague and distorted. Too far to see. I snapped back into my body.

I reported my findings to Sherbet. He said something about me being handy to have around. I agreed enthusiastically. Next, we both felt around the wooden wall until we simultaneously found a seam. We kept feeling until we found a small notch in the wall. Sherbet stood back and I hooked a finger and pulled.

The wall instantly opened, rumbling along tracks hidden in the ceiling and floor. Dust sifted down. Cold air met us. Darkness lay beyond.

Darkness lit by supernatural light and infused with the scent of even more blood.

So much blood.

Stomach rumbling and hating myself, I led the way through into the passageway.

43.

I counted seven ghosts.

Some drifted along the dark corridor. Others simply appeared and disappeared, popping in and out of existence. Still others approached us, curious. Most were in their fuzzy energetic state and composed of tens of thousands of shimmering particles of light. Some spirits were brighter than others, and still others were more fully formed. Most, however, were just faint blobs of light drifting down the dark passageway.

Sherbet said, "I keep seeing movement out of the corner of my eye."

"You're catching sight of them, Detective."

"Them?"

"Spirits."

"We're still on that subject?"

"They're still here, Detective."

He aimed his flashlight down the long corridor.

The light disappeared without hitting anything. A lesser man might have been scared shitless. Sherbet only said, "Again, I don't think I needed to know that. Which way?"

The tunnel led in both directions. I followed the scent of blood and pointed to the left.

"To the left it is, then," he said, and led the way, sweeping his light before him.

The corridor was composed of dank wooden panels. I had no doubt that we were following something built a century or more ago, walled off and hidden, and used by only those with secrets to hide.

As we walked along, I slid a hand along the rough paneled walls, risking splinters. I did this not for balance, but rather to receive psychic hits. I'd discovered that energy is stored in a location—in its walls, for instance. For me, all I had to do was touch such a wall to unlock a location's memory. Weird stuff, I know, but it works.

And what I was seeing now wasn't pretty.

Men and women being forcibly dragged along this very hallway. Kicking and screaming and fighting. Horrific scenes and sounds forever recorded—embedded—within these very walls.

I shivered and, with a procession of ghosts trailing behind us, continued down the narrow corridor.

***

In the hallway before us, a partially materialized ghost—a fragment that looked barely humanoid—drifted toward me, unbeknownst to Sherbet.

It swept through Sherbet, who was leading the way and shivered noticeably, and headed straight for me. As it did so, it took on a little more shape and soon I could see that it was a young woman. Or had been a young woman. Like the others, there was a massive gash along her neck.

As I attempted to step around her—stepping through just seemed a little rude—she drifted to one side and blocked my path. She raised a hand. I tried stepping around her again and again she blocked my path.

"Jesus, Sam. You dancing back there?" said Sherbet, turning and shining his flashlight over me. The light went straight through the girl and even caused some of her form to scatter like frightened fish.

"I'm being blocked by a spirit."

"Of course you are. I should have realized."

The wound in the girl's neck was ghastly. Faint but ghastly. She drifted before me, rising and falling on the supernatural currents.

I said, "She's warning us."

Sherbet was about to say something, then stopped himself. I was giving him a glimpse into my thoughts, allowing him to see what I was seeing, through my eyes. I heard him gasp a little. He backed into the wall behind him.

As the old detective was working through his

issues, I reached out a hand and touched the girl's hand. A cold shiver rippled through me, followed by something akin to an electric jolt. I whispered to her, "We'll be careful, I promise."

She was weeping now, into her other hand, and as I held her ethereal hand, which glowed in mine, I closed my eyes and wished very hard for her to leave this dark place, to leave and never return. When I opened them again, she was gone.

"Jesus, Sam," said Sherbet, holding his heart. "You've got to warn a guy before you pull a stunt like that. I damn near wet myself."

"Sorry," I said absently. "Let's go."

He led the way forward and soon we came upon the same wooden stairs I had seen in my vision.

"I guess we go down," said Sherbet.

"Would be my guess," I said.

"And away we go," he said, and led the way down.

44.

At the bottom of the stairs there was another door.

A light shone from underneath. More spirits were here. A lot more. I counted nine. Many were appearing and disappearing through the door. A few looked back at me.

"This is it," I said, whispering.

"How do you know?" said Sherbet.

"Trust me."

It was all I could do to control myself. Yes, I've had cravings in my life. Sugar cravings. Food cravings. When I was pregnant with Tammy, I had ice cravings.

This...this was no craving.

This was a hunger. A yearning. A need. I shielded my thoughts from Sherbet. No man should hear such thoughts, especially a man I liked and respected.

So much blood, so much blood...
So fresh, fresh, fresh...

Truth was, I had never been so close to so much blood. So much fresh blood. So much fresh human blood.

I heard Sherbet's thoughts as clear as day. He was wondering why they would dump the bodies when the bodies could be disposed of down here. He had just decided that perhaps the killers enjoyed playing a cat-and-mouse game with the police when we both heard a noise from behind the door. The sound of a man grunting. Perhaps lifting something. Sherbet cocked his head, listening.

And that's when a girl screamed.

Sherbet jumped backward, startled. I didn't jump. I kicked. I lifted my sneaker and kicked in the door as hard as I could.

45.

Oh, sweet Jesus.

The sight, although overwhelming, was not unexpected. Two human corpses hung upside down from the ceiling, suspended by ropes. Both were naked. Both had their throats cut open.

Both had been completely drained of blood. The gashes in their necks had been cut all the way to the bone, nearly decapitating both men. They were heavily bearded. One had a lot of tattoos. Both were likely homeless men.

Oh, sweet Jesus.

My knees threatened to give. Hell, my whole world threatened to give. If I had needed to breathe, I would have been gasping. I probably would have fainted, too. Sherbet stumbled in behind me, making a strangled sound. But he kept it together.

We both spotted the men with the girl at the same time.

"Get the fuck down, motherfuckers," said Sherbet.

There were two of them—the same two I had seen creeping around in my backyard. One was holding a wicked-looking knife. They had begun to make a run for it, but thought better of it. The one guy dropped the knife and got down.

The girl was sitting in a chair and shivering violently. Shivering because she was completely naked. She was also maybe eighteen years and if I had to guess she was a runaway: bruises on her body, needle tracks along her inner arm. She was whimpering and rocking hysterically.

So that's how they did it. Prostitutes. Bums. Or those without family and homes. Anyone who wouldn't be missed.

From deeper in the room, I heard the sounds of running feet and someone cursing.

"Get him, Sam," said Sherbet, nodding toward the sounds. "Get that piece of shit."

Now I was moving, flashing quickly through the cold room, around the hanging corpses, around a corner, and down a short hallway—

Where, at the far end, Robert Mason was opening a door.

I picked up my speed. The walls swept by in a blur, and I slammed into the ex-soap opera actor so hard that I drove him through the partially open door and into the room beyond, tearing the door from its hinges. We landed in a heap, with me on top, and I didn't stop punching Robert Mason and that beautiful face of his until I felt his cheekbones shatter.

46.

It was late. Or early.

I was sitting in the theater seats, in the middle row about halfway up, watching the spectacle unfold before me. Medical examiners poured in and out of the theater. Detectives interviewed theater workers.

According to snatches of conversation I was hearing, many bodies had been dug up within an adjoining dirt tunnel.

People came and went. Witnesses came and went. Reporters came and went. Covered bodies came and went.

I sat in the row of seats alone, watching all of this unfold before me like a macabre play. A play just for me. Except there was no plot. No lead character. Just an endless procession of dead bodies.

I had considered calling Kingsley. And I would, soon enough. Once I had processed what was going on around me. But I was missing something here. Something wasn't gelling.

Everything seemed so matter-of-fact. So seamless. No hysterics. And why was no one interviewing me? Other than Sherbet giving me a quick update, he mostly ignored me, too.

It was almost as if I wasn't there.

As I sat and watched, cradling my jaw in my hand, seeing again and again the image of the drained bodies hanging in the air, someone sat next to me. I turned, startled. It wasn't easy to sneak up next me.

There was, of course, only one person that I knew who could pull it off.

Although Detective Hanner's eyes were looking at me, I sensed she was also aware of all the activity still going on before us, too. Her eyes were always a little too wide, always a little too alert, as if she herself were always in a mild state of surprise. Too wide, too wild. There was something close to a fire just behind her pupils, too. Something that seemed to burn with supernatural intensity. Maybe only myself and those like me could see it, I didn't know. But it was there. These were not human eyes. She stared at me and did not blink. Not for a long time, at least.

I waved my hand toward the action on the stage. "You are a part of this."

"As are you, Sam."

"I don't know what you're talking about."

"You have partaken of many who have been

slain here, Sam. Do not deny that you knew otherwise."

"You told me the blood was from willing donors."

"Some more willing than others, Sam. You knew this. I told you this, often."

"You did not tell me you killed these people."

She tilted her head a little. It was not a human gesture. It was, if anything, something alien. "I did not kill these people, Sam. I was a buyer only. And, perhaps, an active supporter." She grinned and spread her hands. "Of the arts."

"You covered up his crimes."

"Of course, Sam. He was of value to me and our kind."

"Sherbet knows," I said. "I told him about you."

The fire in her eyes briefly flared. "I know, Sam. I've removed the memory of your conversation." She motioned to the others moving across the stage, the policemen, detectives, medical workers. "As I have done with all here tonight. None will suspect our involvement, or the involvement of our kind. In fact, most are not aware that we are sitting here, watching them."

"But how?"

"It's not very difficult to do, Sam. With a little training, you could do the same. Especially you."

"What does that mean, especially me?"

"You are particularly...gifted."

"I don't understand."

"You display a wide range of...abilities."

"I thought all vampires do what I do."

She shook her head. "You thought wrong, Sam. Very few can do what you do, although most of us possess typical gifts."

"Typical gifts?"

"The ability to influence thoughts and change minds, minor psychic sensitivity, although only a few of us can transform into something greater."

"Can you?"

"Sadly, no. You, my dear, are a rare breed."

"Why?"

She studied me for a long moment. Never once did she blink. "The reason is the person who changed you, of course."

"Who was he?"

"One of the oldest of our kind."

"Why did he change me?"

"I don't know," she said, but as she spoke, the fire in her eyes dimmed a little.

"You're lying," I said.

She laughed hollowly. "Do you see, Sam? Most of our kind would not have detected a lie. Tell me, how did you know?"

"Your eyes."

"What about my eyes?"

"The fire in them...it went out a little, dimmed."

"What fire?"

"Just behind your pupils."

"You can see a fire there?" she asked.

"Yes."

"Interesting."

"Why?" I asked.

"Because I see no fire in your eyes."

"Fine," I said, turning a little more in my seat. "So, I'm a fucking freak among freaks. That has little to do with the issue here."

"And what is the issue here, Sam?"

"The killing of innocent people."

"The killers will go to jail. Sherbet will be a hero. In fact, he thinks he came here alone, that he acted alone tonight, that he stumbled upon the secret door behind the mirror, alone, that he stopped both killers, alone." She paused and stared at me. "He has no memory of you tonight, outside of your phone call to him."

"Jesus. Does Sherbet still know about me? About what I am?"

"Yes, although it was very foolish of you to have told him. I can only go back so far to remove memories, as you will someday discover yourself. Already you are becoming more and more like us, and less and less like them."

"No," I said.

"Oh? Do you not feel the stronger effects of the sun? Are you not able to venture outside as long as you could before?" She paused and actually blinked. "Someday soon you will never be able to venture out into the light of day. Ever. And your hunger for blood—human blood—will become insatiable."

"Stop it, goddammit."

"I will stop, Sam. But then you and I will have

this talk again soon, and you will curse the day that you stopped such a productive output of blood. You will curse the day that something so useful had been wiped out."

I shook, my head, and kept on shaking it.

"I was like you, Sam. A mother. Full of love and hope. Hope that I would someday be normal again. Hope that this would all turn out to be a bad dream. That was a long, long time ago. Now my son is long dead. The hope is long gone. And I am hungry. Very, very hungry."

Solemn voices filled the theater. Police personnel continued pouring across the stage. All looked shell-shocked. All looked numb. Sherbet was speaking to someone urgently. My detective friend never once looked my way.

"There has to be another way," I said.

Hanner reached out and touched my arm. Her fingers were ice cold. "Someday you will see that there is no other way." She paused, then leaned in and whispered into my ear. "Someday soon."

She stood and was about to leave when I said, "So, this is it. You walk away from this?"

"Yes," she said. "And so do you."

47.

I was in the desert again.

This time, a little further out. In fact, about eighty-five miles out. I was in the hills above a small town called Pioneertown. A fitting name if ever there was one. Pioneertown had street names like Annie Oakley Road, Rawhide Road, and Mane Street, as in a horse's mane. Rebellious.

In all, it featured a few dozen homes, a post office and an inn, all of which I could see from my position high upon this cliffside ledge.

Sunrise was about an hour away. My minivan was parked about a thirty-minute hike away. I was sitting on an exposed ledge with no hope for shade. Doing the math, that meant I had thirty minutes to decide if I was going to do this.

And I was determined to do this.

Seven months ago, I had leaped from a hotel balcony. Truly a leap of faith. I was either going to fly or fall. At the time, I had been at wits' end. My kids were gone, my house was gone, and my cheating bastard of a husband was gone. I had nothing to lose. And so I had leaped...and the rest was history.

Now, my life was a little more stable. I had my kids, my house and a boyfriend who seemed to care for me, a boyfriend who happened to be a fellow creature of the night, even if it was only one night of the month.

The desert birds were awakening, chirping in and around the magnificent Joshua trees which were scattered across the undulating hills below me.

Although my personal life had stabilized, something else was unraveling: my physical body. Perhaps "unraveling" was too strong a word. Perhaps even the wrong word. Perhaps the better word was progressing. Progressing inevitably to a full-blooded creature of the night, unable even to step out into the light of day.

But I had to step out into the light of day, dammit. I had to pick my kids up from school. I had to watch little Anthony's soccer practices, even if from afar, even if from the safety of my van.

I had to.

I had to, goddammit.

I couldn't lose that. I had lost so much already. Watching my son play soccer from my minivan was not too much to ask for, was it? It was shitty, yes, but I at least had that.

My feet hung over the ledge. Directly under

ledge was, I think, a small cave, because I could hear critters moving around inside. These days, I didn't fear critters, even the slithery ones with rattles on their tales. Unless their fangs were composed of silver spikes, or their poison of molten silver, I was good to go.

I checked my watch. Fifty minutes until sunrise. I could still turn around and head back to the relative safety of my minivan, which was parked under the shade of a rocky overhang.

So, why had I come out here? All the way out here? The same reason I had leaped from the balcony seven months ago.

No turning back. I was going to do it.

Or I was going to die.

I held in my hand the emerald medallion. The golden disk was nearly as big as my palm. I absently ran my thumb over the embedded emeralds, which were arranged into three roses. A cracked, leather strap was threaded through a small hoop in the medallion.

Behind me soared the San Bernardino Mountains. The east-facing San Bernardino Mountains. If I was going to see my first dawn in seven years, I was going to do it right. I was going to do it high upon a hill, facing east, with nothing—and I mean nothing—blocking my view.

This is crazy.

Already I was feeling the first stages of exhaustion. Already I was feeling a strong need to lie down somewhere comfortable and prepare for the comatose state that was sleep.

Instead, I sat here on the ledge, and, as the eastern sky turned from black to purple, as the brilliant flares of light that illuminated the night for me began to decrease, I knew that soon there would be no going back.

No going back.

Ever.

Forty minutes to sunrise. I had ten minutes to make my choice. I found that I was breathing fast. Filling my lungs and body and brain with oxygen. Except these days I didn't need much oxygen, if any. These days it was an old, nervous habit. A remnant of my humanity.

And what was so great about humanity?

My kids, for one. And daylight, for another.

Thirty minutes. I began rocking on the ledge, forward and backward. If I wanted to comfortably work my way back to my van, then I had to leave now.

Now.

Except I didn't leave. Instead, I continued rocking, continued holding the gold-and-emerald medallion.

I suspected the sun would kill me. Perhaps not right off. But soon enough. I suspected it would quickly render me incapable of movement and, once unable to move, I would just burn alive. In complete agony. Right here where I was sitting.

In twenty-five minutes.

As the sky continued to brighten, my heart rate,

generally sluggish at best, picked up considerably. The wind also picked up, sweeping over me, rocking me gently. My pink sweats flapped around my ankles. I breathed in sage and juniper and milkwood and dust and the bones of the long dead.

Twenty minutes till dawn. I knew this on a sub-atomic level, my version of the circadian rhythm, or body clock. I was deeply tied to the sun. I knew, at all times, the exact location of the sun. I knew without a doubt that I had twenty minutes before the sun would first appear on the far horizon.

Nineteen minutes.

I rocked some more.

Breathed a little faster.

If I jogged now, I could still make it to my van in time.

Never in my life had I felt so exposed, so vulnerable. I might as well be naked in a shopping mall.

No, worse. Naked in a furnace.

The coming pain would no doubt be ex-cruciating.

And all I had was this.

I looked again at the medallion. The gold surface caught some of the lightening sky, reflecting it a little. I recalled Max's one instruction regarding the medallion:

"Unlocking the secret of the medallion is easy enough for those of great faith."

"Great faith? What does that mean?"

"You will know what to do, Sam."

Easy enough.

Great faith.

I will know what to do.

Truth was, I *still* didn't know what to do, and my time was running out fast.

Fifteen minutes. A strong need to sleep was coming over me.

I would have to sprint now. An all-out run to make it back to my van.

Great faith, he had said.

Faith in what?

I thought about that again, perhaps for the hundredth time, as the wind picked up. Two or three tumbleweeds appeared out of the semi-darkness to skitter and roll in front of me far below. The sky continued to brighten.

There was only one thing I could think of doing with the medallion—and that was to wear it.

You will know what to do.

I dipped my head a little and slipped the cracked leather thong over my head and pulled my long hair through. Thoughts of my kids were dominant now. I could not lose them. Not to the morning sun. My kids were with my sister. The long night at the theater had culminated with me coming out here after a shower and quick change of clothing.

Jesus, what was I doing?

The weight of the medallion was heavy on my chest. After a moment's thought, I slipped it inside my t-shirt, where it now lay against my bare chest.

The sky brightened. Birds sang. Lizards

scuttled. Sand sprinkled.

And I was doing all I could to calm down.

If I leaped from the ledge and changed into the giant flying creature that I am, I could probably just make it to my minivan. But I would have to do it now. Stand now and leap.

Now.

But I didn't stand. And I most certainly didn't leap.

The word "faith" kept repeating itself in my mind. I held on to it like a lifeline.

Faith...faith...faith...

You will know what to do, Sam.

Easy enough, he had said.

Well, there was nothing easier than wearing the medallion, right? Nothing easier than sitting here now and watching the horizon.

I rocked and maybe even whimpered.

It's coming, I thought. *The sun is coming. Hurry now. Back to the minivan. Sure, you might burn a little, or even a lot, but at least you will be safe. At least you will not die. At least you will get to see your kids again.*

I rocked and rocked and rocked.

And as I rocked, as I felt the tears appear on my cheeks, as I accepted that everything that I knew and loved could be taken away from me in this moment, I felt something strange.

The need for sleep was dissipating.

I buried my hands over my face. The tears were coming fast and hard. I wasn't even sure what the tears were for. More than anything, I was afraid to look to the east, afraid to settle my eyes on the distant low hills that led on to forever. But I pushed past my fear, and I took a very different kind of leap of faith.

I lowered my hands.

And for the first time in seven years, I saw something that I didn't think I would ever see again:

The upper half of the morning sun appearing on the far horizon.

I felt no need for sleep. I felt no pain. In fact, I had never felt more alive in all my life. And as the sun continued to rise, I rose to my feet and stood on the ledge and shielded my eyes and never in my life had I ever seen something so beautiful.

Or perfect.

The End

About the Author:

J.R. Rain is an ex-private investigator who now writes full-time. He lives in a small house on a small island with his small dog, Sadie. Please visit him at www.jrrain.com.